The Knights of Wade

The Knights of Wade

Michael Strecker

Two-time Tennessee Williams Literary Festival Finalist

PELICAN PUBLISHING
NEW ORLEANS

The word "Pelican" and the depiction of a pelican are trademarks of Arcadia Publishing Company Inc. and are registered in the U.S. Patent and Trademark Office.

Library of Congress Cataloging-in-Publication Data

Names: Strecker, Michael, 1963- author.
Title: The knights of Wade / written by Michael Strecker.
Description: New Orleans : Pelican Publishing, 2024. | Summary: "In this comic novel set in New Orleans in the late 1980s, an inveterate lottery player will risk everything--except gainful employment--to strike it rich. Filled with local-flavored humor, it features engaging, unforgettable characters and a unique plot that offers insights into fate, faith, and the vagaries of life"— Provided by publisher.
Identifiers: LCCN 2023049245 | ISBN 9781455627813 (paperback)
Subjects: LCSH: New Orleans (La.)—History—20th century—Fiction. | BISAC: FICTION / Humorous / General | FICTION / Satire | LCGFT: Humorous fiction. | Novels.
Classification: LCC PS3619.T7447 K65 2024 | DDC 813/.6—dc23/ eng/20231020
LC record available at https://lccn.loc.gov/2023049245

Printed in the United States of America
Published by Pelican Publishing
New Orleans, LA
www.pelicanpub.com

To Jillian, for always believing, and to my brother Jerry for inspiring much of this story and for remaining at the foot of my childhood bed during the long watches of the night

The race is not to the swift . . . nor riches to men of understanding . . . but time and chance happen to . . . all.

—Ecclesiastes 9:11 (NKJV)

Chapter 1

Wade and Charlene met at Catahoula Creek.

It was a strange place with its kidney-shaped beaches that looked and felt as wonderful as any in the world but were bordered by swampy, scrub woods on one side and by a tea-colored, unambitious stream on the other. In the rainy season, the stream swelled to nearly three times its size and looked menacing enough, but since there were no homes or livestock for miles within the green and red Mississippi land around it, it was a false, silly rage—laughable, impotent. The beaches of the Catahoula soaked up the floodwaters as inconsequentially as a kitchen sponge siphoning a spilled glass of milk.

The bluff, where everyone met, stood some forty feet above the surface of the Catahoula in red velvet rust and brown hues, looking like a wall of the Grand Canyon scaled down many sizes. The top of the bluff had been worn to a powdery gray; a mixture of the red clay road that led to it and the sugar beaches below. Huge pine logs, charred and waffle-branded, dotted the area, the remnants of glorious fires that had leapt into the air and rouged the faces of the inexperienced campers who had kindled them and watched the fires rage with fear and joy. Beer cans, some bleached by the sun or turned ashen by flame, others still shelf bright, were as plentiful as promises.

But it was not a couple's place—not a place where you'd go off alone with your love and an Igloo and enjoy some time alone—although, every now and then you'd see a pair trudging back from an isolated stretch along the creek, sunburned and disconsolate as if the effort and pain had not been worth it. It was not a family place either, although every now and then you'd see a family disembark from a dusty station wagon, a family whose size and income prohibited its entry into one of the parks that charged admission. These interlopers huddled on one of the smaller beaches with bed sheets on the sand and a litter of children near the edge of the creek, playing tentatively as if with a toy that did not belong to them.

It was a group place—a place where overgrown teenage boys, some in their late twenties, with ragged, cut-off jeans swung from a rope tied to the upper reaches of the old black gum that stood sentinel at the bluff's edge. The rope would take the boys far and high over the creek's surface, reaching its apex above the deepest,

coolest part of the creek. The boys would answer the
water's beckoning with surprisingly graceful half-gainers
or straight dives, fist first. The girls watched these heroics
with intent and indifference from the beach below. There
were invariably more boys than girls in these groups—
hardly ever a matching number. The girls did not wear
fashionable swimsuits. Catahoula was a place where
you could be fat and very white and still enjoy yourself
around the water. Your legs did not have to be the sleek
extension of your trunk but could be pale or bruised in
places with webs of blue veins.

Charlene was not fat except for her belly, where a sad
ring of flesh had taken up permanent residency around
her navel. Everywhere else she was bone skinny, with
pointy elbows and jutting knees and feet that begged
for mercy. She hated her body. And yet she always wore
the skimpiest bikini—the same skimpy bikini year after
year, 1982, 1983, 1984 and onward. It was a satin purple
model whose sheen surface repelled water in the most
intriguing way, just sloughed it off like a sharp pitched
roof dispatched rainwater. Charlene felt that this water
repelling action was the only worthy attribute of her
bikinied self. When out of the water she always wore a
terrycloth cover-up, a kind of throw rug for her body.
She would tell herself and others that this was because
she had fair skin and feared the sun. But the truth was
that the cloth acted as a shield against others who, she
knew, would despise her frame as much as she did. She

was wearing the terrycloth coverup when Wade pulled in front of her on a smoking and muttering three-wheeler.

"Want to ride the alley?" he asked by way of an introduction.

Charlene blocked the sun with her hand and Wade's face came into focus. His lips were pulled back over large, square teeth in a smirking smile that repulsed and begged for acceptance at the same time.

The alley was a pitted and ragged red scar that ran along the easternmost extremity of the bluff and sloped downward to the beach. Groups of young people would line both sides of the shallow ravine and watch riders bump, hop, and pray as they traveled down the treacherous stretch in all manner of vehicles— motorcycles, jeeps, pickup trucks, windowless station wagons, even a snowmobile some guy from Minnesota brought once. While the riders traversed the course, the onlookers from both sides of the alley rained every imaginable type of obstacle in their path: creek water brought up in ice chests from the beach, waterlogged footballs, abandoned hats, umbrellas, beer cans, waded paper cups, and more. Sometime branches, half-burnt logs, brickbats, or tires were thrown. The goal, for the drivers, was to avoid the obstacles and make it to the end of the alley.

Charlene had never driven on any motorized vehicle that had less than four wheels. They scared her. But for some reason she assented to this stranger's offer. She wound her cover-up tightly around her and slid behind him on the vinyl seat. The vehicle's muffler, its rusted edges, white hot and purple, pulsated an inch below the strut on which she rested her bare foot. They took off with a jerk, coursed through the sand like a knife over frosting, and then vibrated over the section of washboard road that led upward to the alley.

News had spread fast that a rider was approaching, so when the three-wheeler came to the top of the alley, a hedge of people filled both sides as far as Charlene could see as she looked over Wade's shoulder. Groups of teenage boys with slack postures stood flat-footed before rows of water held in all manner of vessels. One haggard-looking man of sixty, tattooed and round-bellied, still hanging with the kids, had rigged a system that siphoned water from the creek through a network of three-quarter-inch PVC pipes. The man sucked heartily on the end of the pipe, turned red-faced, and then looked toward the riders with puffed cheeks and eager eyes.

Squeezing the hand brakes, Wade revved the motor to a high whine and then looked back satisfactorily at the red spray of clay that flew from the spinning tires. The crowd bristled and bulged like a flexing muscle. Charlene's arms instinctively wrapped around Wade's waist.

"Ready?" Wade asked.

That one word carried with it the tart odor of a whole afternoon of drinking. The odor stung her nostrils and registered a dull concern within her. Before she could say anything, Wade released the clutch and Charlene was jerked backward, certain she would fall off the back of the machine. Loud cheering and laughter—much louder than she would have expected—broke out from the crowd. As they entered the alley, water came towards them from both sides, crashing like cold fists against their backs. Most of the water flew widely off the mark, but other shots landed expertly to the delight of the laughing crowd.

The three-wheeler slid easily through these first torrents of thrown water, then came to a jarring halt. Charlene's chin bounced hard against Wade's back, and she tasted chalk as her top and bottom teeth ground together. The belly of the machine's engine was stuck on a great log that was submerged in the thick mud—an obstacle left over from a previous run. A deep pause fell among the crowd, a silence rarely possible in such a large group. It seemed to rob the very air of its vitality and purpose. Not one drop of water fell upon the alley.

The engine whined as Wade straddled the three-wheeler, trying to rock it off the log. The crowd picked up the panic from the sound of the engine and suddenly emerged from its silence as a unified force moving ever closer to their hapless victims. When one arm was raised to throw, all arms were raised. Clods of mud, well-formed for the purpose, rained down upon Wade and Charlene. Several of the clods found the innards of the exposed engine, sizzling as they landed. One clod, dried for several days and rock hard, bounced off Charlene's thigh. Her skin bulged in a spasm of pain. She opened her mouth to scream, and it was filled immediately with water thrown from the shallow of a frisbee.

The crowd had moved into the alley itself now, slipping on the red paste that they had created. At such a distance, even the most gently thrown obstacle was dangerous, the tossed water breathtaking. Charlene saw two men hurrying towards them from the back of the crowd with a dripping hamper of watermelon rinds between them. She squeezed Wade's waist urgently. In the next instant, Wade kicked the log free, and she was jerked back again. Wade, not entirely on purpose, drove the vehicle straight for the crowd, fanning them back to the grassy border of the ravine. As he herded the crowd thusly, a sudden shock of freezing water and ice cubes fell upon both of them, followed by a white flash. The white flash turned out to be a Styrofoam ice chest their assailant had accidentally let go of during the throw. It attached itself over Wade's head and face. This image realigned the dispersed crowd into a surge of gleeful madness.

The youth who had thrown the ice chest slipped and fell, wide-eyed, directly in the path of Wade. The knobby, front wheel of Wade's vehicle loomed over him, came closer and then turned sharply to the right. The boy, a deeply tan youth with dark stringy hair and a concave chest, scrambled to his feet and rejoined the enlivened crowd who now rained buckets of water, beer cans, pinecones, and sand towards Wade and Charlene with reborn vigor. People tore up huge tufts of grass and earth, holding them like the prized, severed heads of their enemies and then hurling them toward the blinded driver and his screaming, crying partner.

The three-wheeler whinnied and spun hopelessly in a circle, seeming to want to escape the missiles and the moment as much as its passengers did, but there seemed to be no way out. On and on the machine groaned in a dizzying circle, a centrifuge under fire from all sides. A well-placed pinecone, thrown with malice but landing with mercy in the center of the ice chest cracked it in half. Wade shook his head like an angry bull and freed it from the two white halves. He then downshifted and raised the vehicle's front tire in a high wheelie. Charlene screamed above the engine and tore at his shirt. The crowd cheered the wheelie and then immediately responded with wild-arm throws, sensing that these were their parting shots.

Wade brought the three-wheeler to the far side of the alley and onto the smooth sand near the creek's edge. The tattooed older man waited there with his siphoned ammo. He unplugged the PVC and emptied a solid stream onto Wade's head. Then he turned his puffed cheeks toward Charlene, gave a watery grin and spat a healthy volume directly into her face.

Charlene shrieked in disgust. Wade gunned the engine and turned around, heading straight toward the crowd again. He broke through the man's network of pipes, a length of which fell and, balanced across his lap, nearly scraped the legs of some of the running crowd as he drove past them. He bumped back over the hard, scrabbled road that bordered the alley and then drove toward the bluff. At the top of the bluff, he turned hard again and skirted the very lip of the precipice, sending several chunks of clay tumbling into the water. Once straightened, Wade shifted quickly to the highest gear and traveled across the hummocks of tough grass that clung tenaciously to the top of the bluff. Charlene had her eyes closed and one cheek flat against Wade's back. The rough ride made her chin quiver and her mouth hang slack. They traveled back over the washboard road, skirted the alley, plodded through the deep sand of the beach and came to a stop along the water's edge. It was only then that she opened her eyes. The first thing she saw was a man standing a short distance from the front of the bike and staring hard at Wade. He was a small man with a crop of tight auburn curls and a fierce build.

"Mackie might have said you could use it, but it don't belong to Mackie," the man said.

He walked directly up to Wade and, for a moment, was blocked from Charlene's view by Wade's frame.

"It belongs to me," the man said. "Me" was joined with a sharp crack and Wade flew from the seat of the three-wheeler onto the sand.

The man stood, looking at Wade and rubbing his fist for a moment. Then he boarded the bike as if Charlene were not even there. She hopped off just as the vehicle was driving away. She found herself in almost the exact same spot where she had met Wade earlier and accepted his offer to take on the alley. She was splattered with mud, bruised, shaken, drenched, spat upon, humiliated, and burnt—her foot had fallen off the strut during one of the turns in that crazy ride and found the white-hot muffler. Wade was propped on one elbow in the sand, looking up at her. His bloodied lip was curled in another smirking smile. He brushed his dripping bangs off his forehead and pressed the hair to the side of his head.

"There's supposed to be a bonfire up on the bluff tonight," he said. "Wanna go?"

Charlene shook her head as emphatically as her dazzled and dizzied state allowed. No. She did not want to go to no bonfire. She did not want to go nowhere but home. She didn't ever want to see this Wade fella's face again.

Six months later she would marry him. That was just how things went for Charlene Perkins.

Chapter 2

Λ group of men, aligned in rows three deep and three abreast stood behind the home of Stewart George, the Grand Knight of St. Andrew Parish's Knights of Columbus Council 3685. The house was constructed of wide, white clapboards and had green shutters. Embedded in the grass of the front lawn was a set of tires, painted white, filled with peat and brimming with carefully placed, "ham and eggs." This delicate, perennial herb thrived in the rich alluvial soil which, like the inhabitants of the land, had found its way down the Mississippi to this reclaimed, drained and annexed swamp known as New Orleans's Navarre neighborhood.

Stewart stood on the steps that lead to his back door—squat concrete ledges with arcs of algae creeping up their sides. From here, he barked orders to the group of men below, each of whom wore a newspaper hat folded loosely in the shape of a bicorne. Stewart communicated to the men through a conically shaped and stapled leaf of poster paper set to his mouth.

"We will approach the altar at the beginning of Mass to the entrance hymn 'Ave Maria.' You'll line up just as you are now. Remember to keep an arm's length between you and the person in front of you."

A thin man with a large, rigid nose and watery eyes raised his hand.

Stewart acknowledged him.

"Yes. Question," Stewart said.

"What if you happen to find yourself in a position where there is no one in front of you?" the man asked. "I am in the front row. Does the arm's length rule still apply?"

The man waited earnestly and at perfect attention for the answer. A trickle of sweat, darkened by the newspaper ink, ran down his forehead and came to rest in a black thermometer bulb at the tip of his nose. There were rumblings of laughter and shifting impatience at the question.

"Jumping Jehoshaphat," a voice said from the rear. "Take *tree* wild guesses, professor."

That would be Jackie—council irritant. He had a nasally New Orleans accent that seemed to be bred specifically for expressing sarcasm and grievances of all manner.

"Good question," Stewart said.

He took the cone from his mouth and shuffled through a stack of index cards he had pulled from his pants pocket.

"Uh . . . well, let's see now . . . if your position is the front row—"

Stewart stopped and put the cone back over his mouth.

"If your position is the front row, you may ignore the rule of keeping a foot space between you and the person ahead of you."

The man who asked the question nodded emphatically.

"Yeah, yeah. Just don't run over da priest, Percy," Jackie said.

Laughter broke out in the ranks.

Stewart, having missed the punchline, stretched his neck toward the back row as if he might visually spot it. He then came off the steps.

"We'll get the cue from the choir director to begin the procession. Remember, onc foot space on the side and front—"

"Except for the front row," Percy interjected.

"You are correct, Percy," Stewart countered. "But you still must commit to keeping evenly paced on all sides. All of you.

"And here we go," he said, sweeping his hand forward and beginning to deliver his directions to the tune of "Ave Maria."

"Re-mem-ber go slow-ly and with dig-ni-teee," Stewart sang.

The legs of the men moved forward as onc; with surprising unity, their frames, distended, bulging and bulky, shifted knowingly and gracefully forward. Stewart moved his head from side to side, conveying the calm deliberateness with which they were to proceed.

"Dis is like some kind of mid-evil torture," Jackie said. "Like dat rat cage dey would put on people's heads to find out if dey was a witch or sumpin'. Why we got to do dis ova and ova in dis heat? Dis is sumpin' altar boys do every Sunday, walk up the aisle. Dey do it fine and some of them's in the third grade and failing. And dis heat, it's worst den purgatory. It's like dat movie in the desert with da good-looking fella. What's his name, Laurence of Olivier? It's like the Sahara. A guy could catch a heart attack."

Jackie could catch a heart attack, Stewart thought. His nearly three-hundred-pound frame was slogging breathlessly through the grass on inadequate legs. The colored Sunday comics, which he used to compose his bicorne, were thinned and pulpy with perspiration. *Peanuts, Beetle Bailey,* and *Garfield* had turned lava and streaked down his face in rainbow rivulets. The walking shorts he wore hitched and switched together with each labored step.

"I gotta go to the bat room, anyways," Jackie said.

Even if he didn't experience an actual cardiac event, all this complaining was bad for morale, Stewart thought.

"Jackie, you've been to the bathroom twice already this session," Stewart said.

"It's a miracle I can go at all," Jackie said. "Don't you know I got a calcified prostate? I ought to be catharized every time I go, by rights, but my insurance won't pay for it."

"Your home health nurse would resign immediately," someone said from the back row.

"Oh, hardy har har. You fellas yuck it up, back dere. Dey use to make fun of St. Thomas of Aquarius, da same way. He was a big fella, too."

Stewart moved up the ranks of men until he was directly beside Jackie.

"The Lo-rd hates a whine-err," he sang as an improvised coda to his instructions.

"Dat so?" Jackie said. "Well, He must really love them parishioners at St. Vincent's cause dey sure ain't got nuttin' to complain about. They Knights got real hats and real swords you could kill a guy with, if you ain't paying attention. We the ones that got to make do. That ain't even a real megaphone."

Stewart took the cone from his mouth and contemplated it, hurtfully. Jackie knew their uniforms had already been ordered. He knew they would soon be as well-attired as any Knight in the Archdiocese. Why did he have to be so . . . Jackie? Stewart repositioned his homemade megaphone directly over Jackie's ear.

"Did you also hear that Fa-ther Grafton found ter-mites in the nave of St. Vincent's and the pest con-trol said the entire struc-ture may be in-fest-ed?" Stewart sang through the cone.

Jackie's eyes widened gleefully at this news.

"The arch-bishop was planning to sp-end his summer resi-dency at St. Vin-cent's. Can any-one name the larg-est parish close-est to St. Vin-cents that has not been visited by ter-mites—a plague from which even pha-raoh was spared?"

"St. And-drew's," Percy sang merrily from the front row.

"Company halt," Stewart ordered, and the troops came

to an abrupt stop. They had moved across the yard and now stood inches from the back steps.

Stewart clicked the heels of his shoes together. Today, his shoes were mere tennis shoes, but on Presentation Day they would be dark leathers shined to a mirror finish. He would snap them together in a hard union that would echo like the crack of a bullwhip through the church. He placed his hand on the hilt of his rapier which was now a sawed-off broom handle stuck through a belt loop but on Presentation Day would be a sheathed sword that would gleam with a glorious finish when he brought it forth.

"Sir Knights," Stewart called through the cone. "Present arms!"

There was a series of soft rustlings of wood against cloth as each man's broomstick was drawn and held before him—nine singular points against the blue sky. The back door to Stewart's house opened. His wife, Dee, walked onto the top step and then pulled back slightly at the sight of the armaments.

"Stew—Oh, Stewart?

She was looking among the crowd.

"There you are. Your brother Wade is on the phone."

Stewart returned his broomstick to his belt loop.

"Stepbrother," he said, morosely.

He patted Jackie on the shoulder before trudging mournfully toward Dee.

"I wish we had real swords, too," he said.

Chapter 3

When Stewart picked up the extension in the bedroom, he was immediately greeted by the demanding voice of the operator.

"Collect call from Wade Terry to Stewart George. Will you accept the charges?"

Stewart closed his eyes.

"Sir?" the operator said.

"Why not," Stewart answered. "Yes."

"Thank you. Hold please."

Stewart heard the click and then the greeting of Wade.

"How goes it, brother?"

"Step," Stewart said.

"Huh?"

"Nothing. The meter's running. What do you want?" Stewart asked.

Wade laughed genuinely.

"Oh, yeah. Right. Sorry, bro. I was just wondering if it'd be all right if me and Charlene came down to see y'all and have a look at the place."

Stewart's face fell like a heartbroken child's, and he shook his head vigorously from side to side.

"Sure, you two are always welcomed. You know that," he said.

"Yeah, that's what I told Charlene. I figure we'll be moving down there pretty soon. I think Charlene's parents are getting a little tired of us living up here, anyways."

"I can't imagine why," Stewart said into the receiver, and then to himself, "Unless, of course, they're human."

An empty gravel truck, its loose rusting tailgate banging against its frame passed on the road near the outdoor pay phone Wade was using. He followed its path absently.

"Those directions you mailed never got here," he said into the receiver.

"I can't imagine why not," Stewart said into the receiver, and then to himself, "Unless they actually needed to be written and placed in a mailbox."

"Well, Charlene's pretty good at directions. Let me put her on and you can tell her."

"No! Wade . . ." Stewart pleaded.

He found it impossible to lie to her. There was something in her, some oblivious vulnerability she possessed, some trust she projected in her flat, disinterested manner that pained him to the heart to betray. It would be like lying to the Virgin Mary. Stewart panicked. He pinched his thumb and forefinger over his nose.

"Please deposit seventy-five dollars in Buffalo nickels for an additional ten seconds," he said.

"Hold on," Wade said. "I am getting some crazy message from the operator."

"Remember they must be Buffalo nickels. The phone knows the difference."

Wade fumbled in his pockets for some change.

"Hello, Stewart?"

It was Charlene. She spoke in an unadorned, stoic drawl. Stewart could see her standing with her head inside the shelter of the phone box, a memo pad and pen ready to take down his lies as genuine directions. She had probably done well in geography in school. The one subject in which she had excelled during a long, struggling effort that undoubtedly ended short of high school graduation. Now she was her family's authoritative source for the documentation and translation of all directions.

Stewart began to pace the bedroom floor.

"Stewart?"

"Uh . . ."

"Wade told me to get directions. I think I can find your place. I went to Chalmette once and that's close, ain't it?"

"I can barely hear you, Charlene. Bad connection. Must be a downed wire. Can you hear me?"

"I can hear you fine," she said.

He began to scan the room for something to support his

claim. He found a can of hairspray Dee had left on the bed. He picked it up and sprayed it directly into the mouthpiece. He coughed convulsively as he walked through the aerosol cloud toward the bathroom. The long cord allowed him to bring the phone well within the bathroom. He dropped the receiver into the basin and turned the faucet on; water poured into the instrument in a fizzing column.

"Sounds like y'all are getting rain."

Charlene's voice came out of the phone as it lay in the basin.

"Terrible rain," Stewart yelled into the basin. "Slashing, biting precipitation with a chance of afternoon hurricanes. Low pressure trough stalled and is sandwiched between a possible polar vortex with tornadic proclivities and a naughty El Niño."

"Uh-huh," Charlene's voice sounded far away, lonesome and lost through the cascading water.

Stewart picked up the phone and walked back to the bedroom.

"A hint of hail. News people standing in water holding their microphones above the torrent. Pelting sleet. People sleeping on gym floors. Was that a cow?"

"I can hear you fine again," Charlene said.

Stewart stood before Dee's aquarium and looked in upon a scene of perfect tranquility. In its green-tinted depths a ceramic diver sent up a steady stream of bubbles as angelfish glided by silently. Oh, to be in that world right now, Stewart thought, just a solitary deep-sea diver bouncing along the seafloor.

"Flash flood!" Stewart said and plopped the receiver into the aquarium.

It swung gently downward in the water, coming to rest on the pink gravel at the bottom of the tank. The fish in the tank, stripped tropical triangles, bulbous goldfish with streaming tails, and minnow slices, took no notice of the intrusion, save to dart in one direction or the other, eyes fixed, tails making the slightest adjustments to compensate for the bright, white receiver.

Stewart placed his face against the glass of the tank.

"Take I-59 out of Mississippi and follow it, traveling south until it merges with I-10. Go across Lake Pontchartrain and keep traveling about twenty miles until you come to the I-610. Take the Canal Boulevard exit and call us from the Texaco station."

Stewart straightened, smoothed the front of his shirt, and walked resolutely out of the room and down their narrow stairway. Dee was waiting at the foot of the stairs for him.

"Stewart, did you throw the phone into the aquarium again?"

"Correct," Stewart replied.

He walked through the kitchen toward the back of the house. Through the screen door he could see the backyard was empty. He could sense it was empty. He turned to Dee who was still standing by the stairs.

"They left. They know what a foul mood you get in when you talk to your brother," Dee said.

"Stepbrother," Stewart said.

"Stewart, please. How long do you think you can keep this up?"

"Knight practice bother you?"

"You know I am talking about Wade. How long do you think you can keep him off this property?"

"My current goal is the five hundredth birthday of our nation. I'm taking eternity piecemeal," Stewart said.

"Stewart, I was there—" she stopped suddenly as she heard Timmy and Amy, their foster children, come in through the front door. They giggled as they clattered through the cramped house, came down the hall, and headed straight for the back door. They squeezed between Dee and Stewart without looking up. Dee called to them as they ran down the steps.

"Stay away from the dirt pile," she said.

"I'll have to spread that soon," Stewart said, contemplating the dark pile of fill snuggled beside the nearly completed garage he was building.

The garage had been built not as a port for their car, but rather as an extra room, an expansion that could be used for any number of purposes—a playroom, a study, a home gym, a workshop. Their house was a good, sturdy, semi-old New Orleans home perched on a foundation of cinder blocks. It was slate roofed with a red ceramic ridge line and swaddled in whitewashed pine weatherboards. His addition would be an energy-efficient, aluminum-sided dwelling, a twin born last and smaller, possessing its own splendid individuality, yet still an unmistakable sibling of the family residence.

When finished, Stewart would have for himself a modest version of the best of two worlds on the property that it had been his good fortune to inherit. The property had been all his until his widowed mother had chosen to remarry late in life, beyond all reasoning and, in doing so, grafted the misbegotten Wade Terry onto *his* family tree.

"I was there, Stewart, in the room," Dee continued. "When your mother, on her deathbed, I mean literally on the bed in which she died, God rest her soul, told you to let Wade and Charlene move into the addition."

Stewart grimaced.

"Well, mother always did have trouble pronouncing her vowels and remember how she would roll her *r*'s in that clumsy manner. Given that and all the anesthesia and the emotions of the moment, I'm not really sure what she said. Is anybody? She could have been asking for the remote."

Dee spread her arms in exasperation.

"They were her dying words. She was not asking to change the channel. Do you think people at that moment—oh never mind! If you can live with your conscience, I suppose I can."

She turned away and Stewart walked quickly out of the back door. This was a good time to get that dirt spread. He felt the slight rush of finally getting to this pending task of reducing that dark form into neat, raked patches at each low area among his green grass.

"Live with it on *my* conscience," he thought. "Why should *I* feel guilty if my mother was TV-obsessed until her last breath?"

Chapter 4

The attorney wore thin-lensed glasses with reddish brown frames. The glasses stood out from his face impudently, taunting. He was young and was already used to getting his way and getting paid for it.

"It is my understanding that you have not been complying with the wishes of your mother in regard to your brother," the attorney said.

"Step," Stewart said before shooting a hard look across the room to Wade. The weight of the look roused Wade from the copy of *People* magazine he was reading. Donnie and Marie Osmond graced the cover of the magazine under the headline: "Siblings and besties!" Wade gave Stewart a "well, you know" shrug and returned to his reading.

It was Charlene's daddy's idea to go to the lawyer in the first place. Wade wasn't going to burden himself with defending this decision. He didn't like law offices, anyway. All that varnished wood, leathery furniture, and napped carpeting reminded him of a funeral parlor. Wade would have been content to wait until Stewart furnished him with proper directions to his and Dee's home. He did wonder why, for a postman, Stewart displayed an astounding ignorance of street names, addresses, or even the cardinal directions of his hometown. But, as it turned out, Wade instead had to give Stewart directions over the phone to the lawyer's office in Mississippi.

"Stepbrother," Stewart said, looking from Wade back to the lawyer.

Dee kicked him in the ankle. She was seated next to him in one of the two high-backed chairs that faced the attorney's desk. The lawyer swiveled in his own higher-backed chair, showing them one side of it that was filled with a single file line of upholstery nail tacks. He pulled out a low drawer and brought forth a sheaf of stapled papers. He faced Stewart and Dee directly.

"The will," he said. "You'll notice, Mr. George, that your mother attached a qualifying amendment, signed, dated, and notarized, which specifically enjoins you to provide your brother access and full use of the addition you have made to your primary domicile."

Only domicile, you imbe*cile*, Stewart thought. He took out his own glasses, dark bordered things that had been sat upon, lost for days beneath a work bench, radiated when he had forgotten to remove them for a dental X-ray and nearly melted by the sun when he left them on the railing of his front porch one summer afternoon. They were crooked and looked cartoonish on his face. He began to read:

> To Whom it May Concern:
> I, Lorraine Charbonnet George Terry, being of sound mind and body, do this 19th day of January, 1988 hereby state and declare that the permanent deed to my property located at 5335 Greenwood Street in New Orleans, Louisiana and the accompanying dwelling be granted to my heir and son Stewart Anthony George with the sole proviso that an additional building on the adjoining, contiguous parcel, namely, a structure measuring approximately 50 x 50 feet, built for the purposes of storage/recreation be bequeathed to my stepson Wade Oliver Terry for the purpose of providing shelter for him and his spouse Charlene Maria Terry.

At the end of this typed paragraph was a handwritten message in his mother's emphatic script: "Don't try to crawfish your way out of this one, Stewart."

Stewart placed the will on the lawyer's desk and removed his glasses, folding the misaligned temples onto one another.

"Well, having no legal training, I am really at a loss as to what any of this means," Stewart said. "Is there a layman's version?"

The attorney leaned far back in his chair and cocked his head.

"Mr. George," he said. "They do have courts, you know."

"*Mother!*"

That was Stewart's reaction when he finally realized there was absolutely nothing he could do to prevent Wade and Charlene from moving into his beloved addition. A court battle would be costly, lengthy, embarrassing, and, ultimately, in vain. The evidence, the preponderance of facts, was weighed against him. He supposed that they had waited, his mother and her friend (he had never approved of the marriage and could never grant Wade's father a title as dignified as stepfather)—they had waited all during the years of Wade's profligacy, knowing that somehow steady, trustworthy Stewart would devise something—a device, scheme, or opportunity—to rescue Wade from the entanglements of his own mistakes, his long periods of idleness punctuated by moments of fruitless, fading industry. Mother and friend visited New Orleans one day and viewed the skeleton of the addition behind Stewart and Dee's home. If he pondered it enough, Stewart was certain that he heard one, or more likely, both of them let out a pleased, "Ah . . ." as they viewed the addition. Hadn't they rubbed their palms together and exchanged knowing glances?

"*Mother!*"

Surely, his mother and that friend of hers had reasoned in their own demented way that the value of the property and the house in which Stewart had been raised and to which he had moved after his widowed mother moved out to join her new husband in Gulfport was worth the labor and money Stewart had put into the addition. Surely, that addition could better serve as a cute little starter home for the struggling newlyweds. Surely, Stewart would protest strenuously but could do nothing about it, legally, if Lorraine Charbonnet George Terry, being of sound mind and body, were to make that a condition of Stewart's continued habitation of his childhood home and, better still, have her lawyer draft such condition into the will.

"Mother!!!"

Stewart loved his mother, he truly did and, up to this point, he loved lawyers—he truly did. Their unremitting exactitude and commitment to the lettered law, their service to stricture and precision, their florid, archaic language and deference to ancient proscription—these he greatly admired. It was ironic then that he hated this particular attorney—the only one with whom he had ever spent any measurable time—with an epic hatred. From that day forward, that anger spread and settled upon the entire species of attorney, from Edward I to Perry Mason.

All his meticulous planning for the addition, the labor he had expended to create a perfect space of his own would be debased by the din and confusion, the posters and lava lamps (he bet), the noise and tumult of the new tenants and their precarious and unstructured lifestyle.

Didn't the attorney know this? Didn't she know this?

"*Mother!!!*"

The word rang out from the upstairs bedroom from which it had been issued and reverberated throughout the house. It spilled out of the opened windows and bounced along the sidewalk. Neighborhood children, at a playground two blocks away skidded to a stop on scooters, broke their swinging in mid-arc, paused their ball game and stared up at the sound. A dog sniffed the air. A murder of crows, startled by the pronouncement, decamped from the branches of an oak tree and flew in a long circling arc against the blue sky.

"*Mother!!!*"

Stewart emerged from the bedroom, serene, as the last echoes of his outburst banged into the furniture and settled among the corners and curios of their home. He descended the stairs with dignity. Dee and the children sat in the living room, looking at him without expression.

"Well, wife, beloved foster children," he began bravely. "It looks like we are going to have new neighbors."

Chapter 5

Stewart had worked for the postal service for twelve years. He did not like it one bit and, yet, he had not lost his affection for its uniform. Uniforms, Stewart had decided, were one of the defining features of higher human civilization. They signified order, certitude, and the clarity necessary for a functioning society. He was unequivocally the postman as he strode in his blue postal shirt, with sleeves creased and starched to blades, the postal emblem proudly displayed on his right shoulder, his trousers with their wide seam stripes, also pressed to perfection, and his specially arched walkers clicking along the sidewalks.

If it were up to Stewart every occupation, without exception, from garbage collector to US president would have its own uniform. That way you could know all about a person, or all you really needed to know about them, within seconds of first meeting them. It was likely the uniform that kept Stewart working for the postal service for so long despite his dislike for the job. Or perhaps it was the stability or the fact that the tasks of this particular career, which were terrifyingly complex in his first months on the job, could now be accomplished largely by rote, leaving him plenty of time for thinking. How lovely it was to let his stream of consciousness ebb and flow freely as he walked the well-known pathways of his route: the solemn, mustached cashier at the corner 7-Eleven, the passion with which Mr. Liberto, at 2821 Fleur de Lis, tended his mirliton garden, Dee, Vietnam, World War II, Knight practice, Mass, Dee, Vitamin C's multi-generational popularity, the letter t, the number 8, chipped ice versus cubes, Timmy, Amy, rabbits, ice cream, Dee.

At times he would attempt to arrange these thoughts into organized groups and clothe each individual thought with its own little uniform: ordered, discrete, understood. This attempt was shattered the Monday after their visit to the lawyer when that torpedo of a thought—that Wade and Charlene were actually, at any diabolical second now, moving into the addition—exploded across his mental vision. He misdelivered five letters that day and threw Mrs. Murphy's TV Guide, the one with Dick Clark on the cover (that showoff) into a drainage canal.

Mercifully, he was spared being present for the initial arrival of Wade and Charlene. They showed up outside his home, after receiving vivid instructions from the attorney, one late Wednesday afternoon when, as Stewart liked to note, decent folk were working. Stewart, Christian pilgrim, was embarking on the final leg of his route. Dee, having just returned from her teaching job at

St. Raphael's, gave them a tour of the house.

"Nothing shabby about y'all's taste," Wade said, looking appreciatively over the living room.

He was wearing a faded yellow tank top and polyester red pants that had been cut in a seismographic pattern at the knees. He appeared pudgy and loose beneath the silk material of the tank top. His skin seemed too weathered and strained for a man who had celebrated his twenty-sixth birthday only two months ago. He habitually brushed a swath of his brown-blond hair off his forehead with the fingers of his left hand spread widely apart. This elaborate act accomplished little as the hair returned, persistently, in an unmanageable clump just above his eyes.

"The flood didn't do much damage, huh?" Charlene asked, vacantly.

"What flo—oh," Dee said. "No, it was, uh confined to a small area. Localized, as they say. Would you like to see the upstairs?" she added quickly. "It's tiny up there, but cute."

As they walked up the narrow stairs, Charlene took notice of the rows of framed pictures of Timmy and Amy that ran along the stairway wall.

"How long do you get to keep them?" Charlene asked.

Dee was ahead of them on the stairs and only half heard her.

"How long do I see who?" Dee asked.

"No," Charlene said and motioned to the pictures. "Them kids. They ain't really yours, are they?"

Dee rubbed her hand against the top banister.

"That's right," she said quietly and hated the answer.

This was the plan. Wade and Charlene were to move in that weekend. Although unfinished, the addition was still livable. It had running water, electricity, and a window unit. Wade, who had worked intermittently as a carpenter's mate, could build the partition walls, finish the ceiling, tile the floors, and install the bathroom fixtures. In the meantime, they could shower in the main house. This is what happened: Wade and Charlene moved in that weekend. Although unfinished, Wade came to believe the addition was fine just the way it was. It had running water, electricity, and a window unit. Ergo, Wade did not build the partition walls, finish the ceiling, tile the floors, or install the bathroom fixtures. He did, however, put in a small wet bar. In the meantime, they showered in the main house.

"They're really not motivated, are they," Dee said to Stewart one evening as he worked on the final draft of a letter to the editor of the *Times-Picayune*.

"Dee, did you remember to fill out and mail that order form for the Knights' uniform for me?" Stewart responded.

"Yes," Dee said.

"And you sent along the check from the Knight's account. The same cumulative amount of the individual checks we had received from the Sir Knights?"

"Yes," Dee said.

"Did you note, as marginalia on the form, that the uniforms must arrive at St. Andrew's no later than the twenty-fifth? Presentation Day is on the twenty-seventh and the mail is always slower near the end of the month, due to a surge in remittances, catalog orders, and other circumstances completely out of the control of your average letter carrier (no matter his or her diligence), so the deadline has to be the twenty-fifth."

"Yes," Dee said.

"You didn't go through any of these new couriers, I hope. These Fed Exes and UPS types with their little Nazi uniforms could put the good old post office out of business, that is what I say."

"Yes, that's what you say," Dee answered.

She had just ironed her cute floral top for school and was now working on his postal uniform. Year round, even in the torturous New Orleans summer, Stewart insisted on wearing the long-sleeved postal shirt with the aforementioned blade creases, starched cuffs, and placket as stiff as a ruler. Short sleeves, Stewart had decided, were for the beach. In cooler or winter weather, he wore a British airmen's sweater he had ordered from the special selection pages of the official postal uniform catalog. He had the only one of its kind at his postal station.

Stewart suddenly stopped his writing and turned in his chair.

"Who isn't motivated?" he asked.

"Wade and Charlene," Dee answered.

Stewart looked about his desk, which was actually a square kitchen table he had brought from downstairs when their new dining set had arrived.

"I am searching for my desk calendar," he said. "The one State Farm sent us. Easel-style, free-standing. Very small, but functional. Ah, here it is! I want to mark that down as the understatement of the year. We are only in July, but my guess is second place won't even be close."

Dee plopped down on the bed and sighed.

"They just don't seem to be able to adjust," she said.

Stewart picked through some other papers on the overwhelmed desk and handed one to Dee. It was titled, "A Grief Observed: Complaints Against My Stepbrother and Stepsister-in-Law." It included 120 items.

Dee began to read.

"Stewart, this isn't fair," she said.

"Which one?" Stewart asked.

Number thirty-five.

Stewart's lips moved silently as he recalled the exact order.

"Ah," he said. "Show me one shred of evidence that they are not planning a revolution. He drinks vodka all day and she sews flags."

"She makes quilts," Dee said. "She sold three of them already. They're pretty."

"They are poor!" Stewart said.

"Well, yes, I know. But if they could just catch a break—"

"Not them. The quilts," Stewart said. "They are poor. They yell it out in big, bright colors, 'We are poor!' They're sold to poor people who use them to cover up their poor sofas or beds, or sofa beds more like it. Or the occasional rich person might buy one thinking, mistakenly, that they are some kind of folk art."

Dee ignored him and read on, scanning to the bottom of the page and turning it over to the read the back.

"Okay, seventy-four is true. Seventy-five, seventy-six," she laughed. "Seventy-seven. Oh, Stewart if the kids ever found this . . ."

That was seventy-eight.

"It's all documented," Stewart said. "Now, here, read my letter to the editor."

Dee handed the complaint page back to Stewart and took the letter from him.

"You may have misspelled the word 'malodorous' in your 'Grief Observed' page by the way," she said.

Stewart frowned.

"Number ninety-eight," he said looking at the page.

Dee began to read the letter to the editor.

"Out loud, please," Stewart said.

Dee rolled her eyes, cleared her throat, and read aloud the following:

"Dear Editor:

Regarding the response to my letter on the demise of the Oxford comma and the End Times . . ."

Chapter 6

The mid-morning sun scorched his eyelids. He knew he should open them but, oh, the consequences. If only he could return to the repercussion-free slumber he had enjoyed for, how long? Eight, ten, twenty-four hours? The surface of his back rested against what was definitely not his bed. He could hear outside sounds, too, including that of nearby passing traffic—a cause of alarm for any waking sleeper. Finally, he came to the firm resolve that he would open his eyes in twenty seconds. Exactly.

"One Mississippi, two Mississippi, three Mississippi, four Mississippi, five Mississippi . . ."

He slept for two more hours and then, waking with a start, bolted upright. His legs dangled over the edge of an estimable height. He, it turned out, had been reposing in the shallow of a large satellite dish on the sparse, gravel pitted lawn outside an establishment known as the Trader's Lounge. Wade put one hand to the sun and surveyed his predicament. He patted himself to make sure all his clothes were on and that they were all his. Check.

"Not bad," he decided.

He slid out of the dish until his feet touched solid ground. He steadied the quivering surface of bowl, before stepping away. He then began a tentative journey along the sidewalk. His head felt like it belonged to someone else who had died long ago and was now mummified. His stomach was an empty balloon of distant rumblings and peculiar longings. He suddenly stopped and came down heavily upon a raised brick border that surrounded what might be called the landscaping of an insurance business next to Trader's. His head landed among scrub junipers and discarded soda bottles. He was about twenty feet from the satellite dish.

"Must be something going around," Wade said, massaging his forehead. "In bottles."

To be fair, this was the first real stinker he had thrown in a week. Before then, he had been adequately imbibing at his own home bar and honestly seeking to further his career goals or, more correctly, his career goal. He had only one: to win the "New York State Lottery." It had to be "New York State Lottery" because that was the only lottery game sold, at the time, within Orleans parish and the only one broadcast on local television. A satellite dish, similar to the one he had recently awakened from would have, of course, greatly expanded the number of television stations Wade could have consulted for winning announcements. But Stewart had vowed to hack "into one million pieces" the one that Wade had had the temerity to order, via Federal Express no less, and which had arrived by that courier service at Stewart's very doorstep one late Saturday afternoon.

"Does this mean you aren't going to sign for it?" the disinterested courier asked.

"Kindly remove this parcel, your person, and the lingering spirit of that ridiculously rhetorical question from my property," Stewart said. "If you need directions out of the neighborhood, just ask the nearest letter carrier," he added as the courier shrugged and began to cart the package back to his truck.

Turning back toward his house, he spied Wade returning to the addition from whence he had exited upon seeing the arrival of the Fed Ex delivery truck. Stewart followed him across the driveway, two narrow strips of cement, and into the addition.

"How, pray tell, did you expect to pay for that?" he demanded. They were both standing before a great burgundy colored quilt with a giant yellow starburst radiating from its center. Throughout the addition Wade had tacked Charlene's quilts from the ceiling, cordoning off sections of the dwelling into vaguely distinguishable rooms.

"He's so good at carpentry," Charlene had told Dee at the end of this project. "You really need to come and see it."

"Bro, there's such a thing as layaway," Wade said. "Ever heard of it?"

"Step-bro," Stewart retorted. "There's such a thing as justified homicide, ever heard of it?"

Wade laughed.

"Good one."

"How can a person with no visible means of support even consider making such a purchase?"

"When I win the New York State Lottery, I will be using satellite dishes like that for soup bowls," Wade said.

"That's *if*—a gigantic, ginormous, and yet infinitesimally insignificant whiff of an if," Stewart said.

Wade brightened again.

"Did you make that up?"

"I—"

Timmy poked his head from under a quilt.

"Mr. Wade, it's on."

"Step Mister" Stewart said. "And what are you doing here anyway?"

"It's fun here," Timmy said, dropping the quilt over his face and disappearing.

"I'll bet," Stewart said, lowering himself stiffly down to crawl under the quilt. Once on the other side, he stood up in near total darkness, except for a small cube of light coming from a television set resting on the floor. Stewart felt along the draped walls with his hands and moved tentatively towards the light.

"Tent dwellers," he mumbled. "Give me four solid walls and a dead bolt."

"Over here, Mr. Stewart," Timmy cried. "Hurry, its starting."

"*Masterpiece Theater?*" Stewart asked.

Wade was seated in a low rocker directly in front of the television. Timmy was kneeling close to the rocker, straining to read the figures he had written on a sheet of loose-leaf paper. Charlene was propped up on something—it was too dark to tell what—the red glow of a cigarette highlighting her indifferent stare.

"Mr. Wade's numbers are two, twenty-two, three, fifty-two, ten, and sixty-six," Timmy said.

"Wonderful," Stewart said. "Sure winners—individually or as a team."

Banner music emitted from the television and the screen was dotted with a variety of numbers. The figures filled the space and then swirled away, coalescing into a thin line that then expanded and emerged into the block letter tittle, *Lotto Luck.* The camera panned to a smiling host standing in front of a giant lotto form. In front of him was a large plexiglass cube half-filled with numbered ping pong balls.

"Good evening and welcome to *Lotto Luck* where just a few minutes can change a life forever. My name is Peter Barber and if you've been watching *Lotto Luck* regularly you know the possible winnings for this week have accrued to forty million."

The host pointed to a red button at the side of the cube.

"Depressing this button will activate our fraud-proof process for selecting tonight's winning numbers. The air, ladies and gentlemen, does not lie. Shall we begin?"

The host pressed the button and the balls in the tank suddenly came alive, popping over one another in response to air jetting from the bottom of the cube. In seconds, one ball had emerged from its swirling fellows and landed into a holding area at the top of the cube.

"Number ten," the host said. He took the ball away from the holding area and placed it in a clear cylinder at the top of the cube.

"That's one, Mr. Wade!" Timmy shouted.

Another ball was thrust into the holding area. The side facing the camera showed plain white. The host turned the ball with his thumb and forefinger until it revealed a dark number eighteen."

"Number eighteen," the host said.

"That's another," Timmy said.

Stewart, who moments earlier had made an imperceptible motion to leave, made an imperceptible move to stay.

"Number twenty-two," the host said.

"Whoa, another," Timmy said.

Wade nodded his head slightly. Charlene took a long, affirmative drag from her cigarette. Stewart wanted to say, "Well, this is ridiculous. I am not wasting another minute of my time . . ." But instead, he only flinched. But this time perceptibly.

"Our fourth number is zero-three," the host said. "That's zero-three."

"That's another one. Wow!" Timmy said.

The right side of Stewart's face pulled into a series of fluttering spasms.

"Number fifty-two," the host said.

Timmy bounced up and down on his haunches.

"Mr. Wade, that's another one!" he exclaimed.

Stewart snatched the paper from Timmy's hands. He squinted in the dim light to read each number carefully and then looked up at the screen and found its video twin. Only one numeral remained to be called and the series would be complete.

"Are these in the right order?" Stewart asked, waving the sheet.

"Order don't matter," Wade said.

Stewart looked at the screen.

"Sixty-six. Sixty-six," he mouthed.

But no ball shot into the holding area. In fact, all had ceased their popping and settled onto the floor of the cube like a stack of orphaned eyeballs. The host looked into the camera.

"We'll reveal this evening's final number after these messages."

"Communist!" Stewart hissed.

They suffered through an interminable cavalcade of advertisements for acne cream, a high fiber cereal, a record and tape club featuring Dick Clark, that show-off, another high fiber cereal, this one which mildly aroused Stewart's interest, and an exclusive offer for a low interest credit card for which Wade had already sent in his application. Midway through the last commercial, Wade fished the remote control somewhere from his seat and switched the channel to a baseball game. Stewart let out a low whine and began moving towards the television set.

"Just wanted to see what my Cubbies were doing," Wade said and flashed back quickly to *Lotto Luck.*

The host was giving a summary of all the events that had led up to the selection of the final number which, in just moments, would be revealed.

"Now, if Jana would be so kind as to assist me in picking the final number . . ." the host said.

A smiling blonde created, it would seem, for the sole purpose of selecting tonight's winning number came onto the stage.

"Who is Jana?" Stewart asked.

"Jana is our guest selector this evening on *Lotto Luck,*" Peter Barber said. "She will have the honor of choosing the final, and possibly winning, number on tonight's show. Jana is a graduate student," the host said. "Studying?"

"Communications," Jana chirped. "I—"

"Do—"

Both the host and Jana laughed.

"Go on," the host said.

"I was just going to say that I wanted to say 'hello' to my folks in Schenectady to whom I owe so many of the opportunities that have come my way . . . " Jana said.

"That's very sweet," the host said. "I am sure they must be very proud of their daughter. Do you come from a large family?"

"Let the vixen press the button," Stewart bellowed.

Wade turned in his chair and gave Stewart a smirking smile. Charlene coughed a wet smoker's cough that turned into a laugh. Timmy jumped whenever Stewart raised his voice.

"The youngest one is three. Ashley," Jana was saying. "She says she wants to go to college so she can be a football player."

The host threw back his head in an appreciative chuckle.

"Well, with those goals, I'm sure she'll go far indeed," the host said. "Now are you ready to select tonight's final number?"

"No. No. Let's hear more about Jana," Stewart said. "All this time together and we still don't know her Rh factor. It seems like only yesterday she came on stage."

"I told my folks this morning that I really felt that I would choose a winning number," Jana said.

"Well, winning is what we're all about, Jana. That's what *Lotto Luck*'s purpose is," the host said.

"Or is it to kill me?" Stewart said.

"It's all in your hands, Jana," the host said and motioned to the cube.

Jana nodded and pushed the red button. The eyeballs at the bottom of the cube swirled to life again and began popping over one another.

So did Stewart's.

"And the final number in tonight's series is sixty-six!" the host said. "No! Seventy-six. Seventy-six. Seventy-six. Seventy-six. My apologies. I hope I didn't stop any hearts out there. Seventy-six."

Stewart's heart had stopped.

Wade, who had leaned forward when the number was called, now eased back into the chair and switched the channel to the Cubs game.

"Oh, well. You only need to win once," he said.

"It's the top of seventh and the Cubs are tied with the Astros 6 to 6," the game announcer said. "No, I'm sorry, that's 7 to 6. The Cubs are winning 7 to 6. Hope I didn't stop any hearts out there. Ha. Ha."

Stewart opened his eyes.

"Come along, Timmy," he said. "All this darkness is not good for bone growth."

"Bye, y'all," Charlene called, rough-throated from her seat. Had it even registered to her how close she had come to being a multi-millionaire?

Stewart walked unblinkingly out of the room, mowing down one of Charlene's quilt walls. This brush with fortune was not enough to win Stewart over to the numbers game.

"It is just wild luck," Stewart later told Wade, after the latter had tried to use his near miss of the jackpot to justify his somnolent lifestyle. "You can't let wild luck be the basis for your entire life."

"Everything in life is luck," Wade said, giving that smirking smile, which Stewart had decided was not a mere smirk but more of a mocking reaction to standardized, normal living.

"*Lotto Luck* is just honest enough to call itself that."

"Honest!" Stewart said. "I'll bet Jana and her parents are divvying up that forty million this very minute. Little

Ashley now has aspirations to own a football team."

Many lottery players—some who had won, most who hadn't, picked a set of numbers and stuck with them for years, hanging doggedly onto the digits even when the numbers didn't come close to winning. Ever. Or they used a combination of birth dates and anniversary dates and favorite numbers. Wade smirked at this. He believed that winning numbers were actual, tangible things that existed somewhere and must be actively pursued. This perusal was the one work-related activity he did with unremitting diligence. He searched anywhere numbers could be found: on license plates, cash receipts, playing cards, scoreboards, vodka bottles (they're there) book binders, album covers, and, most recently, telephone poles.

In fact, this is what he was doing now as he squinted through the fingers of his right hand, which was shielding the sunlight. There was a yellow metal band about eight feet from the base of a telephone pole with six figures stamped into it. Wade took a tattered memo pad, the size of a small index card, from his back pocket and copied the numbers down with the stub of a pencil. There were a dozen or so telephone poles along the street. Wade would scribble down whichever of the numbers moved him, spoke to him. It would take a heroic effort to work through this hangover, but he intended to do so. And to be fair, his choice of drink the previous evening had been domestic beer. If he was a revolutionary—at least he was an American one.

Chapter 7

There were two things that really peeved Stewart George. There were innumerable things that made him angry, indignant, enraged, agitated, steamed, miffed, red about the ears, irate, piqued, galled, choleric, wrathful, incandescent, and mad. But only two things could really consume him, like a nagging itch burrowed deep in a leg cast that so vexes one that it is impossible to continue functioning without first addressing the grievance. One of the two things was people reversing his name and calling him George Stewart. And, worse, not even apologizing when corrected but commenting something along the lines of, "Oh, well, it could be a name either way," as if his nomenclature were some kind of horrible outdoorsmen's vest that could show either hunter's camouflage or a dressy navy blue to the world. Good heavens.

The second bane of his existence was popular music. He

despised the entire genre and not for the reasons many despised it. He did not find its volume or intensity particularly offensive—its screeching guitar or cacophonic drums lines disturbing. He was not concerned with the "backwards masking" he had heard about in which popular bands allegedly embedded Satanic or otherwise naughty messages within the vinyl grooves of records— messages that could only be discerned when the album was manually spun backwards. Frankly, he was more concerned with the way his name sounded backwards than anything the producers of modern records might slip in between the grooves. No, what charged Stewart's irritant cells to overload was the banality and frivolity of it all—the utter lack of substance to this music, which was supposedly the soundtrack of his generation. Ugh.

He believed it was quite possible that a foreign power would infiltrate the nation's borders, become popularly elected and impose a totalitarian form of government upon the land of liberty while its inhabitants, rocked, rapped, got down and/or boogied. As a direct result of his great disdain for popular music, Stewart listened to it more than either of his foster children, most teenagers, and many record producers did. The music annoyed him that much. Recently, he had noticed Amy beginning to take an interest in pop music and Timmy, on the cusp of entering junior high had, of course, become enamored of all that was androgynous, angry, on fire, and unkempt in the rock world.

Stewart and Dee's weekly trips to the supermarket afforded a perfect opportunity for Stewart to attempt to instill in Dee a baleful, felonious opinion of contemporary music. He had begun to accompany Dee to the grocery without fail these days in order to enforce the strict regulations he had imposed on food purchases for Wade and Charlene. It had been six months since those two had moved into the addition and, by this time, the Georges had begun paying for their grocery bill. This practice did not develop overnight but, as Stewart observed, like any vice, it took hold by degrees. First, Dee invited Wade and Charlene to dinner. Then Charlene, wanting to return the favor, invited Dee and Stewart over for Saturday lunch. Stewart sent his regrets. He had to stay home and repair the phone. Dee accepted the offer and was shocked by the bare spaces in Charlene's makeshift cupboard—a haggard, sagging bookshelf of peeling paint she had salvaged from someone's driveway. It was populated by lonely cans of pork and beans, orphan packages of ramen, crackers shattered to crumbs within their packages, dented vegetable cans, contorted shapes of fast-food ketchup packets, and a large jar of peanut butter with a tin foil lid. Dee partook gratefully of the paltry offerings and nudged the kids under table to do the same. The next evening, she invited Wade and Charlene over again for dinner. They then became expected regulars and when Wade's unemployment benefits dwindled and the sale of Charlene's quilts became too infrequent, Stewart was moved (by Dee) to provide the addition dwellers daily victuals.

But he didn't give up without a fight. The night before each grocery trip, Wade would appear at Stewart's door with a list of his and Charlene's needs. Stewart would take a pen and immediately delete the following categories:

1. Anything featured on a television commercial before noon on a Saturday.
2. Anything not edible, i.e., *TV Guide*
3. Alcohol and all its derivatives and antecedents, including vanilla extract

If there were any specifications on the list, such as a certain brand of cereal or a particular width of sliced bread, Stewart would be sure to purchase the exact opposite of this product. If they wanted orange juice, Stewart would buy them apple juice. If they wanted a specific type of pork sausage, he would buy them a certain kind of sliced ham. Tylenol? Bayer. A TV dinner for two? Frozen pizza for one. Fresh ground coffee? Instant tea. Frosted Mini-Wheats? Spoon Size Shredded Wheat. Mounds? Almond Joy. Scratch that. No treats.

Stewart had the stereo of their red Colt programmed to the three stations he hated the most. He would drive along with Dee at the wheel while the radio's speakers whispered song after song. Then when a pristine example of the corrupting trifle was played, he would suddenly hush Dee and turn the radio up to nearly full volume.

"Listen," he cried suddenly as they were on their way to the grocery one day.

Dee swerved at the jolt of sound. The words of a Jefferson Starship hit rose up from the plastic grating of the front speaker.

"Listen!" Stewart shouted again, leaning forward to turn the radio even louder.

This song was one of the most pernicious of the lot and he could not believe his good fortune in having it come on in the presence of Dee.

"I would willingly burn to ashes now, if you'll stay with me," the singer crooned.

Stewart looked at Dee for agreement.

"I would willingly burn to ashes now if you'll stay with me," Stewart said. "Well, I guess that means no second date."

"Oh, Stewart," Dee said.

"Just imagine what kind of attitude this type of drivel could instill in the children," Stewart said. "Imagine Timmy at a job interview. 'Well, I would like to say I could start on Monday, but there's this girl I really like and, well, I might set myself on fire between now and Monday morning. It's a long weekend.'"

Stewart pressed the dial, and the digital numbers began switching toward the station he had programmed.

"The Bay," he told Dee. "Wait 'til you hear some of their vinyl vexations."

A loud commercial came on for a "hot legs" contest at an establishment named "The Lakefront Party Barge."

"How would you like Amy entering one of these

tournaments?" Stewart shouted above the sound.

"Amy is ten years old," Dee shouted back into the wall of sound that surrounded them. "She doesn't want to have her legs judged. She wants a John Denver album."

"The cowboy?" Stewart said. "What is his deal, anyway, always doing those specials with The Muppets. What's in it for him—a young fellow like that hanging around a bunch of dolls."

Dee looked out the window and then back at Stewart.

"They aren't dolls . . . they're . . . and John Denver is not so young. He's been making good music for a long time."

"John Denver," Stewart said. "Do you think that is his real name. He sings about 'Rocky Mountain High' (a drug reference, by the way) and his last name is Denver. What are the chances? Shhh . . . listen!"

Stewart turned up the radio to its absolute maximum volume.

Cyndi Lauper was frantically singing over and over, "There's a hole in my heart that goes all the way to China."

He turned the radio down after a few verses when he noticed Dee keeping time to the beat with a slight movement of her fingers on the steering wheel.

"Now, I ask you, is that a proper lyric for a future mother?"

"Cyndi Lauper is pregnant?"

"I'm talking about Amy," Stewart said.

Dee laughed.

"I think you may be rushing things a bit. She hasn't had

any seriously proposals yet."

"Well, I will speak my mind about that when the time comes," Stewart said.

"I have no doubt you will," Dee said without conviction, knowing full well that, in all likelihood, they would not still be fostering Timmy and Amy when that time had come.

"Listen!" Stewart cried again and turned the radio up once more to full volume.

Suddenly, there was the piercing sound of tires squealing against pavement. Dee jolted to a stop in the middle of the intersection. An oncoming car she had not seen, a dark, wide, blue sedan buckled to a stop not two feet from the driver's side door. Dee, who realized she had run a red light, raised an apologetic hand to the breathless driver and passenger of the car. After a moment, she drove away silent and shaken through the blaring of horns from other cars. They continued down the road, passing a public park bordered by a low, rusting chain link fence and a broken sidewalk. A brood of pint-size soccer players in bulging knee pads and high socks were struggling with a ball between two closely spaced goals. The ball seemed to be the common foe of both teams.

"When I was ten," Stewart said, looking at the children.

"You what?" Dee snapped. "Listened to Dvorak around the clock? Composed your own concerto? What level of high-minded morality and erudition had you attained? Were you gainfully employed? Had you orbited the earth?

Cured a disease? Addressed the U.N.?"

Stewart said nothing but looked into his side mirror. He could see the same sedan that had nearly collided with Dee just a few seconds before. The driver was an older, extremely tidy and well-scrubbed looking gentleman—probably a retired executive of some sort. His wife was an attractive woman, whose age had just caught up to her regal bearing. They were now driving in the same direction as he and Dee and looked as if they were still recovering from the incident. The driver was commandeering the car in a tentative manner far below the speed limit. They were slipping further from Stewart's view.

It had been a very close call—and he and Dee's only words since then had been bitter. What if the driver had been a little less alert and had driven full force into the metal of Dee's door? At that speed and angle, she would probably have been seriously injured or worse. He heard the tires of both cars screaming again against the pavement. He took his gaze from the side mirror and shut off the radio. He tried to shut out the sound and sight of the catastrophe they had just barely avoided, but it played again and again in his head with fresh terror. They drove in silence for some time until the car rocked slightly as it entered the incline of the store's parking lot.

"I can't remember what I had done by the time I was ten," Stewart said. "I hadn't met you, yet. So, what does it matter?"

Chapter 8

Stewart secured the gauge over the valve stem of the tire. A steady stream of air passed over his fingers, reverberating and shuddering the pads of his fingers. He readjusted the gauge slightly until the stream was cut off and the white measuring stick, black numbered, shot out the back of the instrument.

"Thirty pounds per square inch, aka PSI," Stewart said.

It made sense that the Colt, which was driven five miles to the post office and remained parked in its lot all day while he worked his route and then driven five miles back home, would not lose much air from its tires. Still, recently Stewart had begun to feel a drag on the acceleration of the car and the troubling sense that he was travelling with a flat.

"Thirty pounds per square inch, aka PSI," Stewart said, as he checked the next tire.

"Maybe it's something with the transmission," Sid Edwards said.

Sid, whose mail case stood next to Stewart's in the sorting room, had just come up behind Stewart in the parking lot. His postal jacket was slung over his folded arms, and he snapped a small piece of gum in his mouth.

"It's not the transmission," Stewart said, leaning over another tire.

Sid pressed the piece of gum against the roof of his mouth and popped a series of descending bubbles.

"Heard about the route change?" he asked.

Sid was well aware of the trouble Stewart was having with his brother (or was it his stepbrother?) and sister-in-law having moved into the addition. He took an unconscious delight in adding one more straw to his friend's load.

"Thirty pounds per square inch, aka PSI, yet again," Stewart said. He straightened and looked at Sid. "What route change?"

"Jenkins is moving inside at the end of the week. Window clerk. Guess who's going to get route thirteen."

"No!" Stewart said, heatedly. "I've got more time than Tyler or the Knave."

"The Knave is moving inside at the end of the week, too. He found out that you call him that, by the way, I think he may like it. Anyway, Tyler's quitting. He'll run the route for one more week. Then it's all yours, baby," Sid said.

Route thirteen was infamous among the letter carriers

because of one particularly quarrelsome and unyielding customer who resided at 3114 General Haig Street. His name was Sir Henri. He was a very large, very male boxer/mastiff/bulldog mix—and he was very hungry. Jenkins had been doomed to stay on route thirteen for so many years due primarily to the fact that he was a hopeless dog lover, who refused to complain, take legal action, or even categorize Sir Henri's nearly weekly attacks upon his person as anything other than the well-intentioned but perhaps overly playful overtures of a rascally pooch.

"Oh, no, never mind," he said to the general stir that arose the time he came into the post office dripping blood from his right forearm. "Sir Henri just got a little excited today."

"No, that's okay," he said when asked by Postmaster Gravier if he wanted to file a formal grievance with the USPS's legal office after Sir Henri had sent him scurrying into the bed of a pick-up truck parked in a neighborhood driveway. When the dog had followed him into the bed of the truck, Jenkins was forced to scramble onto the roof of the cab and finally had to jump onto the home's carport roof, receiving a wide, red burn across his belly that had scabbed over and split painfully for weeks.

"Oh, no, never," he said, after a coworker suggested he sue Sir Henri's owners to compensate for the pain and suffering he endured from the ankle he fractured coming off a high curb and into a pothole as he raced toward the safety of his mail truck with an unleashed and unhinged Sir Henri hot on his heels.

It was a heart attack that finally moved him inside to a clerk job, Stewart would later learn. It was a mild one that Jenkins was not even aware he had experienced until presented with the incontrovertible evidence following a routine physical. A fifty-one-year-old man with a bum ticker could not continue to fend off the assaults of a four-year-old dog, the doctor told him.

"Get an inside job," he said. "And I would sue the owners of that crazy dog. His attacks probably brought this condition on."

"Oh, no," Jenkins said, shaking his head and smiling.

"Oh, no," Stewart said, shaking his head and frowning.

"I thought I would brace you for the news before Mr. Gravier told you," Sid said, now feeling a slight pang of guilt that he dismissed as indigestion.

He threw his jacket over his shoulder revealing a coiled magazine in his left fist. He tapped Stewart's chest with the magazine and began walking away.

"See you, Stew," he said.

"Bye," Stewart said weakly.

He waited by the Colt for a few minutes before walking towards the post office to receive Mr. Gravier's confirmation of all that Sid had already told him.

Stewart strained a bit as he turned the container of

liquid mace, breaking the clear plastic seal that enveloped both cap and can. With the seal broken the cap came off easily. He placed the nozzle of the can into the top of a battery-operated and extremely real-looking Uzi-style water gun. When the can was empty, he tossed it aside and picked up a fresh one, repeating the process. The gun held four cans. He slipped two shiny batteries into the gun's clip with a solid, sinister click. Stewart held the gun before him, nodding approvingly as he contemplated its contours.

"Patty Hearst would have been proud to brandish this," he said.

He then kicked back on his and Dee's bed with one hand propped behind his head. The other hand held the Uzi. He squinted one eye, aimed, and fired. A long stream of mace shot across the room and landed on a photo Stewart had taped to the center of an oval, full-length mirror in the corner of the room. The photo was a blurred polaroid of Sir Henri in mid-attack. Stewart had taken the photo through the mail truck's driver's side window yesterday. The unprovoked assault came near the end of route thirteen, far from Sir Henri's accustomed feeding grounds. Stewart had taken the photo for Exhibit A of what he hoped would be a successful lawsuit should Sir Henri catch him off guard one day and he was the one coming into the post office with blood dripping from his forearm. The photograph was extraordinarily incriminating, its blurred image accentuated the maniacal approach of the animal, its predatory instinct—teeth bared and fanged, the purple gumline protruding beyond the snarled lips, jutting out like a claw machine, almost separate from the animal, ears set flat against bristled fur.

Stewart had planned to keep the photograph in a folder which would soon be joined by more evidence in an iron-clad indictment of Sir Henri's viciousness. (He intended to represent himself when the time came for litigation, unable to stomach the thought of paying an attorney for anything.) Then he had discovered the Uzi in the toy section of K&B's and decided to take the law into his own hands, in another sense.

After his first shot with the Uzi, Stewart rose from the bed and examined the photograph. He smiled at the big drop that covered Sir Henri's nose.

"What's the matter, Hank?" he asked. "Catch a cold? Sudden doggy asthma attack? You're wheezing something awful."

He moved back and forth in front of the photograph.

"That's it. Breathe deeply. Get that phenacyl chloride distributed evenly throughout your respiratory system. What's that? You need to get it off your skin? Well, come on big fella," Stewart motioned with his hands as he backed away from the mirror. "Here's some nice St. Augustine. It's a shade grass that requires very little maintenance, even in harsh Louisiana summers. Give your nose a good rub. That's right don't stop until you hit pay dirt. Keep it up. Harder."

Stewart suddenly grew quiet. His countenance turned solemn, his body upright and rigid. He held the gun across his chest.

"You have taken your last bite out of the US Mail, or this US male, Sir Henri," he said.

Chapter 9

Stewart arrived at the post office early the next morning, sorted his mail in half the time he normally took, and was on his route, his new, lucky thirteen route, before 9:00 a.m. He held high hopes for engagement with the enemy that day. When he entered the top of General Haig Street, Sir Henri's home turf, a wave of barking arose, beginning with the toothless yapping of the Schexnayders' ancient dachshund and continuing down the street like an activated piano roll. But Sir Henri's sharp, pistol crack of a bark was conspicuously absent from the chorus.

"How's the hunt for Scooby Doom going?" Sid asked when Stewart returned to the post office at the end of the day.

"I saw neither hide nor hair of the brimstone beast," Stewart said dejectedly. "You don't think that heartworm-laced porterhouse Tyler tossed him last week might have taken him out already?"

"Fat chance," Sid said. "Tyler went soft at the last minute. Never did drop the bomb."

Stewart took his mailbag off his shoulder and placed it on the brass hook next to his mail sorting case.

"The DeLeos are probably on vacation again," Sid said. "No kennel will keep that thing, so I heard when they go out of town, they just throw a caribou carcass or something next to a trough of water in the backyard and keep Sir Henri locked up back there. Even his majesty cannot scale that fence they've built. I don't know how they got a permit for that thing."

"Me, Henri, and my little friend alone in the backyard," Stewart said to himself. "I like those odds."

Sid was leaning over to retrieve a key he had dropped.

"How's that, Stew?"

Stewart jolted back from his reverie.

"Huh? Nothing," he said. "Hey, Sid, you think you could give me a lift home?"

"Sure," Sid said.

They began walking towards the exit, weaving through the maze of stacked parcels and ink-stained gunny sacks straining with tomorrow's mail.

"Vehicle still disabled?"

Two mornings earlier, the Colt had made a strange, spurting noise when Stewart had tried to start it, then it hummed, moaned really, in an eerily mechanical/human way and then fell silent—unmoved by his vigorous turning of the key and wild pumping of the accelerator.

"Yes," Stewart said. "Wade, my stepbrother, is supposed to be working on it."

"Oh, is he good at cars?"

"Oh, yes. His work comes with a one-hundred-proof guarantee."

Mr. Gravier opened the door to his office as they passed. He looked at Stewart open-mouthed and hesitant.

"Crazy question. But you're not delivering your route armed with a machine gun, are you?"

Stewart frowned and tilted his head.

"I didn't think so," Mr. Gravier said. "I've got some lady on the phone here who says—"

He closed the door without finishing the sentence and picked up the receiver he had laid on the top of his desk.

"No, ma'am." Stewart heard him say on the phone. "I just questioned the carrier who delivers that route. Yes, he is new to this route."

Pause.

"Well, I don't know for certain," Mr. Gravier, said. "But I am sure that carrying a machine gun on your route would violate postal code. I don't like to point fingers, but could it have been a delivery person from one of the couriers such as FedEx? They do dress an awful lot like our postal carriers."

Chapter 10

The house next door to the DeLeos' had remained vacant since its renovation nearly a year ago. It stood in virginal solitude among the other well-kept homes along the street. Its eaves were straight and sleek, the interior wall paint still shaving cream white and reflected in the high gloss of the empty, newly refinished wood floors. If one would enter that sealed tomb of a home, the colliding odors of new wall paint and varnished flooring would be intoxicating.

Stewart wished he could enter. Instead, his reflection was sprawled, tilted, and elongated over the front windows of the home as he skulked his way to the safe side of the DeLeos' imposing privacy fence—which was not a fence at all but a stucco brick wall, more than ten feet high. As Sid had observed, even Sir Henri himself could not surmount such an edifice. When Stewart came to what he judged to be the middle of the wall's length, he stopped and positioned himself in front of a thumb-sized chink in the wall. Sir Henri was at the far end of the yard, his back to Stewart, lying in the dust beneath an oak tree, gnawing a large, white bone.

"Marrow of the newspaper boy," Stewart mumbled.

He looked up; just above him, slightly to the right was a block column of wall topped by a granite plate. Standing on tiptoes, he threw the strap of his mailbag around the post. He pulled to test its strength and snugness. He hiked his left leg up until he found a toehold in the chink. He gave a pull and a push and in seconds was straddling the top of the fence wall. From there he could hear the lively salivating of Sir Henri as he worked the bone over in his mouth.

Once, the dog stopped mid-bite, lifted his head quizzically and gave one sharp bark—a questioning, a warning. Stewart's heart rose high in his chest. When the dog returned his attention to the bone, Stewart swung his one uncommitted leg over the wall and slid down onto the moist grass of the DeLeos' backyard lawn. Taking the Uzi from his mailbag, he crept forward, his shoes sinking noiselessly into the thick carpet of grass. With each step forward, Stewart grimaced. A snapped twig or stumbled-upon yard rake, even an errant ball, would mean disaster—death by chomping. Keeping the Uzi in front of him, he made steady progress until he was a mere four feet from the dog. Then he stopped. He watched as the sides of the animal, beat in rapid spasms of asthmatic breathing against the dust beneath it. The movement had a winnowing effect on the dust, pushing it into two little ridges beside the dog's bulging rib cage.

"Boo!" Stewart shouted.

Sir Henri's shoulders stiffened and thrust forward. Clearly, he had been startled.

Stewart laughed heartily.

Sir Henri recovered quickly and turned slowly around facing Stewart with what could most accurately be described as a smile. The bone fell from his mouth.

Stewart jumped back theatrically and then began to run at half-pace.

"Oh, help me! Help me. Good gracious, help me!" he cried in a breathless falsetto. "There's a mad canine after me. *Chien fou!*"

He turned his head and looked at Sir Henri, who followed at a confident, knowing gait.

"Oh, he's one of those boxers mixed with a mastiff and just a dash of Doberman, I bet. They're bred to be ill-bred. They'll make a pit bull look like Pluto—the Disney character, not the dwarf planet."

Stewart wrung his hands above his head.

"I'll never reach that wall on time and even if I did it would be like scaling the Rock of Prudential—the actual 1,300-foot Rock of Gibraltar, not the logo of the successful insurance and financial management company."

The Uzi bounced steadily against his chest as he ran in place not ten feet from the wall, his hands outstretched in faux desperation to reach it.

"He'll surely sink those big white fangs directly into my—"

Stewart bounded to the wall in a single leap, spun and turned just before making contact with it and then bounced his back off its hard surface. He came face to face with Sir Henri.

"Heel," he said as he positioned the Uzi in front of him and readied himself to fire.

Sir Henri, in turn, positioned himself for the first and final lunge.

Stewart aimed the Uzi directly at Sir Henri's face. Sir Henri growled and bared his teeth. Stewart squeezed the trigger.

Nothing happened.

He squeezed a second time, even harder and a trace of liquid emerged from the barrel of the gun, filled the small indentation near the end of the barrel and then dropped silently, invisibly, onto the grass at his feet.

Frantically, Stewart probed the inside of the Uzi's clip and felt only air.

"Batteries," he said weakly and promptly passed out.

Sir Henri crashed headlong into the wall where Stewart's jugular had been a moment before. He bounced off the wall and shook his head. For the first time in his life, his bulldog face looked as if it had really been mashed up by impact. He eyed the empty wall curiously, appraised the prone figure before him and then instinctively began to bury it. With his back towards it, he furiously unearthed segments of lawn, dirt and leaves and heaped them onto Stewart's legs, chest, and face. This was about the time that the cleaning lady came to rescue. She had entered the DeLeos' home just moments before and, for no particular reason, looked into the backyard. She immediately bounded out of the rear door, yelling for Sir Henri to come to order. Except she didn't call him Sir Henri. She called him "dog." She had been cleaning the DeLeos' home for two months now and hadn't learned that dog's name. Didn't care to learn it. Knew it was "Sir" something or other, but she didn't call no dog "sir." No sir. She and her husband had operated a storefront bar in Central City for twelve years. Its front windows were painted black to keep the sunlight and the cops out. On the black background of the windows, her husband had painted in an unskilled hand, "The Second Chance Lounge: Pool, Beer, Liquor, Checks Cashed." In her time as a proprietor of that joint, she had to deal with customers a lot tougher than this old, mush-faced dog and she never called any of them "sir." Not a one.

"Hey, dog," she yelled as she came out of the house.

Sir Henri looked at the powerfully built figure headed his way and frowned—affronted for the second time that morning. Just as his lips began to snarl and pull back over his teeth, the cleaning lady came down upon his head with her broom. She made sure the bundled bristles at the very top of the straw broom made the first impact. She hit him a second time and a third time on the rump as he ignominiously retreated.

Stewart was awakened to the sound of brisk sweeping. The cleaning lady was sweeping dirt, grass, and twigs off him. She noticed his open, frightened eyes.

"Mailbox is in front of the house," she said. "Right next to the doorbell. Got a little fleur-de-lis on it and all."

"Where is Sir Henri?" Stewart asked.

"That fool?" the woman said and jerked her head to the side.

Stewart looked in the direction to which she had jerked and saw Sir Henri gnawing once again on the white bone. Stewart jumped to his feet, eyeing Henri with each movement. The woman continued to sweep him.

"I should inform you, madame, that we are both in danger of becoming dog food," Stewart said. "Can you make a tourniquet?"

"That dog ain't gonna hurt nobody," she said and frowned at a particularly stubborn patch of soil on Stewart's British airmen's sweater.

"Still, I'd feel a pinch more comfortable if I were on the other side of that wall."

"The only exit is through the house. I don't know if I should let a stranger into the house. Not sure the DeLeos would like that very much. Not sure I would like that very much."

Stewart was confident that he could locate the foothold again and, employing his mailbag strap, surmount the wall once again. But the thought of turning his back on

Sir Henri, the cleaning lady's confidence notwithstanding and batteries not included, filled him with a torturous dread.

"I'm not a stranger," he said. "I'm your friendly neighborhood mailman. A public servant."

The cleaning lady had not stopped sweeping him off.

"My mailman don't dress this nice," she said. "Is this wool?"

She was admiring his airmen's sweater.

"It's a blend," Stewart said. "You can get them with your uniform allowance. Most of my coworkers don't bother because they don't care how they look or they would rather buy around one hundred summer uniform shirts instead of one durable sweater. Will you please stop sweeping me?"

The woman took the broom away, turned abruptly around and headed toward the house. Stewart followed tentatively behind her, not sure at all whether he would be granted admittance or not.

"I've got a loaded .38 in my cleaning bag," she said over her shoulder. "The front door is straight ahead, once we enter the rear foyer. I never heard of a mailman who didn't know the mailbox was in the front of the house. But you do dress nice."

"I actually don't see one shred of humor whatsoever in the entire incident," Stewart said.

Sid was leaning halfway out the driver's side of his minivan, emitting a wheezing noise as he attempted to suppress another round of spasmodic laughter. His shoulder belt was the only thing keeping him from plummeting to the pavement below.

"I could have easily been eaten," Stewart said. "He was burying me. That is what the larger predators do with kill. And then that housekeeper threatening to shoot me with her gun. It was all very traumatizing." He ran a hand over his face.

Sid ran a hand over his own face. He sat up straight and promised himself he would not laugh again. In all seriousness, it was actually a dangerous situation and, while nothing even remotely comparable to this had ever happened to himself or anyone he knew or whom he had read about, he could certainly relate to the frightening and tragic aspects of the incident as a fellow human being, a coworker and a friend.

Okay.

He cleared his throat and was about to ask Stewart something related to the subject but not touching directly upon any of the objectively hilarious moments of the incident. But when he went to form the first word, he was struck with a mental image of the dog burying Stewart or his little Uzi malfunctioning or the woman sweeping (sweeping!) Stewart and he would fall sideways against the van's door, wracked in actual physical pain from laughter. No sooner would he tamp down one round of laughter and, with earnest resolve, try to begin anew his conversation than he would be slayed again, tripping another mental humor mine and exploding into laughter.

"Drive. Drive," Stewart said, finally. "Please just take me home."

Amy and Timmy sat blinking in the cool evening twilight that flickered through the next-door neighbors' crepe myrtles. Stewart carefully backed the Colt down their ribbon driveway outside of their home. Wade had finished working on the car that afternoon.

"Solenoid," he had said to Stewart as he pluckily handed him the keys. "It's working fine now."

It was working fine now. Stewart leaned his head out of the car window and adjusted the steering wheel as he watched the tires respond, snaking against the strip of concrete beneath them. He stopped when the rear tire on the driver's side was in the direct path of the Uzi water gun (batteries not included). Stewart had placed the gun there. He shifted the Colt into neutral and eased his foot off the brake. His aim was perfect. The gun at first resisted the weight of the vehicle. Then its edges turned white and the whole frame of the gun fractured and flattened. Its liquid ammunition, still unfired, squirted from the blown sides of the gun and ran down the driveway. When he was certain the gun was completely destroyed, Stewart drove the car back up the driveway and repeated the process three times. He then killed the engine and exited the vehicle.

"Now, children, I think we all learned an important lesson about how to treat a malfunctioning and unreliable product. Any questions?"

Timmy raised his hand.

"Yes?" Stewart asked.

"Can we go eat now?"

"You may," Stewart said.

Timmy and Amy hurried inside. Stewart leaned against the car, folded his arms, looked at the darkness descending through the twisting barren limbs of the crepe myrtle and sighed heavily. He could have been eaten.

Chapter 11

That Sunday was Presentation Day, the twenty-seventh of February. Stewart had called the church office on the twenty-fifth and spoken to Tommy Harris, the venerable longtime custodian of St. Andrew's.

"I'm looking at them right now, Mr. George," Tommy said in his piping voice that often seemed to border on extinction, wavering as it did and nearly vanishing during long sentences.

"Hold on, Mr. George," Tommy said and placed the phone down on the top of the uniforms. Each uniform was individually, hermetically sealed within a clear plastic bag. Tommy lifted each package and moved his lips silently. When he reached the bottom package, he straightened and picked up the phone.

"Ten, Mr. George. Yeah, they look real nice. Hold on."

Tommy put the phone down again and flipped through the stack.

"Yes, sir. Every one of them has a big, long plume like an ostrich feather, and a hat. Real nice. Yeah. Okey-dokey. Bye-bye."

"Oh, wait, Tommy!" Stewart said.

"Hey," Tommy said, pulling the receiver back to his ear.

"Tommy, the rapiers—did they arrive, also?" Stewart asked.

"Yes, indeed," Tommy said. He counted the hilts in the tall cardboard box that leaned against the stack of uniforms.

"Ten of them. Real sharp. Nice."

"Excellent. Thanks, Tommy."

Stewart hung up the phone and clapped his hands together. He walked briskly out of the house and onto the backsteps of his house. The Knights were strewn about the backyard. Several were seated at a picnic table and assorted lawn furniture. Some were enjoying the shade under the overhang of Wade and Charlene's addition, their paper hats pulled low over their eyes, arms resting on their knees. Jackie was lying flat on his back in the middle of the lawn, his paper hat resting on his immense belly like a tiny sailboat on the crest of a mighty swell. Percy and another Knight were engaged in a vigorous sword fight with their broomsticks. As soon as Stewart walked through the back door, Percy looked up and lowered his broomstick to his side. The other Knight, sensing an opening, immediately thrust his broom handle into Percy's belly.

"Ooof," Percy bellowed. "You may have punctured an organ."

The other Knight stood silently, looking wondrously first at the tip of the broomstick and then back at Percy. Stewart picked up his megaphone, which he had inadvertently stepped on coming out of the back door. He straightened the one crimped end of the cone and then put it to his mouth.

"Sir Knights, gather round," he called.

The Knights under the overhang looked up groggily. Jackie lifted his head and peeked over his belly and hat. The Knights at the table shaded their eyes to see Stewart better. Percy took a few staggering steps forward, grasping his injured stomach.

"I am pleased to announce that the order for our uniforms and rapiers has arrived at St. Andrew's Parish Church and will be pressed and waiting for us when we arrive for the Presentation Day this Sunday."

Cheering broke out among the scattered, sweaty ranks. Jackie lifted his thick fingers into his mouth and whistled shrilly from where he lay. Those resting against the addition threw their paper hats in the air. The Knight who had poked Percy in the stomach with his broomstick sword now clasped his hand over his shoulder and gave him a friendly side hug. Percy smiled broadly and then, remembering his pain, winced. When Stewart called the Knights to order, they all fell into perfect formation and obeyed with renewed earnestness the directions repeated to them by Stewart. Privately, Stewart feared that some glitch, some unforeseen obstacle, was going to keep them from ever wearing those uniforms. As he sang his customized chorus of "Ave Maria," he wondered if any of that fear leaked out: "Ke-ep your feet str-aight but not lock-ed. We are Knights not Na-zis."

Though arriving early to church for Presentation Day was foremost in his mind as he counted the days, hours, and minutes until Sunday, somehow, against all reason, Stewart found himself running late for Mass that day. He had never been late for Mass in his life. Seriously. Not one time. And now the most important Mass of his life (he had been too nervous to feel the import of his wedding Mass and was an infant for his Baptismal Mass) was about to commence and here he was still running around the house, half dressed, and ordering the kids into the car. When he came out of the house, Stewart was slipping on his suit coat. His tie, twisted and turned into what closely resembled a French braid, was resting around the perimeter of his forehead. Amy, who was too young to distinguish real tragedy from humor, giggled unabashedly in the seat next to Timmy, pointing at Stewart's head. Timmy kept a cautious eye on Dee in the front seat, looking for cues.

Stewart piled in behind the steering wheel and faced Dee. He pulled the tie over his face and raised his head to allow her fingers to work.

"Why?" he cried.

Timmy jumped.

It was true that the suit was wholly unnecessary since

Stewart would change into his Knight uniform as soon as he entered the church. But he felt that, as Grand Knight, the walk from his car to the church should be attended to with some ceremony and formality of dress. By rights, Dee should be driving.

"You are choking me," Stewart squeaked.

Dee's knuckles dug deep into the coils of his Adam's apple.

"I just want to get it," she grimaced, "straight."

Stewart's face turned red, then purple.

"Watch closely children, this is a good way to learn the prism color scheme," he said in a raspy, fading voice. "Also, you may be called to testify at a later date."

Dee was now kneeling on her seat, putting her finger underneath the tie and pulling it taut. When the encroachment of her fingers reached their most painful point and Stewart began to become lightheaded, she suddenly proclaimed, "There!" She settled back in her seat, satisfied. Stewart took a few hearty and grateful gulps of air, checked the tie in the rearview mirror, gave Dee a nod of appreciation, and started the engine.

Percy's was the first face Stewart recognized when he entered the vestibule of the church.

"Hello, Percy," Stewart said.

Percy received his greeting with a startled flushed face, a gaped mouth and pained expression. He continued walking past Stewart, away from the small office at the rear of the church.

"Nerves," Stewart said, nodding a farewell to Dee and the children and walking briskly in the direction Percy had come. Jackie presented himself to Stewart before he had turned the corner of the narrow corridor that led to the church office. Jackie wore a newspaper hat on his head. For some reason he saluted Stewart.

"The uniforms," he said huskily and then fell silent.

Stewart edged past him and bumped into another Knight. He was wearing a hat made from a glossy advertisement page from that Sunday morning's paper. It pictured torsos of young women in half-priced bras. Stewart immediately snatched the page off the Knight's head and crumbled it into his fist.

He looked around at the Knights who surrounded him in a silent, brooding circle.

"What is going on here?" he demanded. "Why aren't you Knights in your uniforms?"

"Those uniforms aren't ours," Eddie Bartholomew said.

He stepped forward out from the circle of Knights, as if to physically lay claim to the words he had spoken.

"The bank notified the church office yesterday that the Knights' check had bounced. Each individual Knight gave you a check for their uniform, which was duly deposited. But apparently, our books didn't record the Special Olympics camping trip and some other expenditures and our account was in the arrears."

He spoke in a cool, detached manner which fell with equal accusation on each of the assembled Knights, even upon those who had nothing to do with "the books," who were only vaguely aware that such ledgers existed. Stewart turned away from Eddie and looked through the half-open door of the church office. The uniforms lay undisturbed on the pallet on which they had been delivered, openly mocking him. Their mere presence instilled within him a nearly overwhelming desire to dash atop the pallet, draw one of the rapiers, slash the two plastic bands that secured the uniforms in place and begin tossing them to his eager troops. It was a fantasy, of course. He did not do things such as that.

Meanwhile congregants were filing into the vestibule and into the nave of the church. Stewart could hear the cacophonies of the organ that would soon meld into the familiar strains of "Ave Maria." He knew he did not have much time to act. He glanced at a cafeteria-style table set against one wall of the office. On top of the table were stacks of St. Andrew's two-page weekly bulletin, awaiting distribution after Mass.

"Bulletins," Stewart said, pushing through the door. "Everyone, take a bulletin."

Once inside the office, he lifted a handful of bulletins from the closest stack and began passing them around.

"Make your chapeaus out of these. At least they're somewhat ecclesiastical" Stewart said. "And not . . . pornographic," he added as he shoved one into the Knight who seconds before had sported the lady's underwear hat.

The Knights began an awkward and hurried effort to fold the bulletins without a readily available plane surface. Some squatted to the floor, others cleared space on the office's table. Several employed the wall or hiked up a knee. Two took turns using one another's bent back for a folding surface.

"Hey, Patrick Kendall's getting married. Ain't dat nice, as ugly as he is," Jackie said, as he worked his bulletin against his stomach with his chin pressed hard against his sternum.

"Jackie, fold," Stewart hissed.

"Couldn't we just do the presentation without the hats?" Eddie Bartholomew said.

Stewart stopped folding his bulletin. He had worked so tirelessly for the Presentation Day. He had run the image of the Knights in their hats with their fantastic plumes approaching the altar in graceful glides through his head so many times that for someone to suggest they enter the procession bareheaded was tantamount to proposing that they go before the congregation in their underwear. Stewart may just as well have heard the words spoken, "Couldn't we just do the procession in the nude?" His mind flashed back to the underwear ad he had just snatched off the head of one of the Knights. Had his council been infiltrated by sexual deviants? Stewart looked around him. Everyone had stopped folding, awaiting his answer.

"No, Eddie," Stewart said quietly. "I don't think we can do that. It would be like having Mass without the priest."

Eddie cast his eyes down, chastened, as if he had actually suggested such a thing. Stewart looked at the other Knights. One at a time, they returned to their folding, determined to fashion the best paper bulletin bicorne that had ever rested upon a Knight's head. Suddenly, an altar boy with scrubby patch of brilliantly red hair and matching freckles appeared among them.

"Father says Mass is about to start. Y'all ready?"

Stewart was on his last fold, tucking a triangular shaped wedge into a slot at the crest of the hat.

"Yes," he said. "We'll fall in behind as planned."

The altar boy looked at his hat, smiled just a bit, nodded, and walked away. Stewart watched as his head rose and fell in rhythm with his boyish gait. He saw the boy round the great stone column bordered by statues of St. Andrew and St. Peter—a youth among ancients. Undoubtedly, in the next few seconds the boy would whisper Stewart's message into the declined ear of Father Hemmler. Father Hemmler would nod gravely as if he were hearing the last confession of a dying man. Father Hemmler did everything gravely—baptisms, weddings, funerals. He was nearly completely bald, save for two white tufts above each ear. Though tall and rail thin, he still managed a slack double chin that exacerbated the dour, but well-meaning, expression with which he greeted the world.

"Okay, Knights, fall in," Stewart said, hurriedly placing his bulletin hat on his head. "When I call 'present arms' just reach to your side and thrust your right hand toward the altar. Come on, the procession is about to begin."

The Knights made a hurried and undignified dash across the vestibule to the entrance of the nave with Stewart at the head. He settled directly behind Father Hemmler. The rest of the Knights fell into three rows, each consisting of three men, an arm's length apart on the front and sides. The carrot-top altar boy with the freckles was at the head of the procession carrying the long-staffed processional crucifix. He turned around, spied Stewart, and smiled once again. Stewart motioned for him to turn around.

The organ fell suddenly silent. The cantor walked to the podium and leaned toward the microphone that was placed there.

"Good morning," he said. "Today's entrance hymn can be found on page ninety-three of the hymnal. Please rise and greet Christ in our priest, Father Hemmler, as we sing 'Ave Maria.'"

Father Hemmler moved forward as the congregation rose and began to sing languidly. Stewart mouthed his instructions to the hymn's music, hoping the Knight's would telepathically receive them. When the procession reached the front pew, Father Hemmler and the altar boys broke off, genuflected, and took their positions behind the altar. Stewart and the Knights were alone at the front of the center aisle. The hymn ended a verse earlier than Stewart expected and, if you were very close to him, you could hear him singing, "Rem-em-ber we are not Nazis," in a voice that quickly faded when it realized the music had stopped.

"Company, halt," Stewart said in the silent church. "Dress, right. Dress."

The Knights spread out, standing astride Stewart before the altar.

"Uncover, two," Stewart said.

The Knights removed their paper hats and placed them over their hearts.

"Draw, swords," Stewart ordered.

He clicked his heels together smartly. The Knights reached toward their sides instinctively and then thrust their right hands into the air. Stewart looked up at his own hand quivering above his head and then glanced at the other raised hands on each side of him. He blinked.

"We look just like Nazis," he said.

It is difficult to say who laughed first. Stewart had a strong suspicion it was the red-haired altar boy. Others thought it was someone from the choir loft. Or perhaps a recent convert. Regardless, as soon as the first laugh was emitted, allowed and, as it were, sanctioned, the others followed in a deafening roar. Stewart stood his ground. He was unable to communicate with the Knights beside him because of the noise, and he was unwilling to simply abandon the troops and sprint to the nearest exit. Then a series of flashbulbs went off, blinding him. A woman had pushed through her tittering pew and was kneeling on one knee before the Knights, attempting to capture the moment on film. She may have been with the local paper. No, it was Percy's wife. She smiled and waved at Stewart when he looked at her irritably. Then she took another photo.

"Return swords," Stewart shouted above the din.

And this made those parishioners seated nearest the Knights, those who had actually heard Stewart's command, laugh even louder which, in turn, made the others behind them laugh even louder and so on down each varnished pew. Red-faced, but still undeterred, Stewart nodded bravely to the men.

"To your pews, brothers."

"How's that?" Jackie said, "Can't hear ya."

"Go to your pew," Stewart commanded.

Jackie moved towards the pew nearest him while the other Knights slipped into pews filled with family members.

"Not there, that's my pew," Stewart said.

"What it got your name on it or sumpin'?" Jackie said.

"It has my wife in it," Stewart said, pointing to Dee. "Go stand next to your own wife."

"My wife ain't here. She got the croup sumpin' terrible. Or it might be the angina. Poor baby. Gawd's lucky I'm here today, at all."

Stewart looked around. Every pew was filled to capacity.

Resigned, he stood next to Jackie, while Jackie shuffled down to the spot next to Dee.

"Hiya, heart." Jackie said to Dee. "Where the kids? Oh,

dere day are. Gawd, love them. Dey getting so big."

Pockets of mirth still popped out here and there but, for the most part, the laughter had subsided. Still, people were talking the events over quietly among themselves. Men were wiping tears from their eyes with handkerchiefs retrieved awkwardly from back pockets. One teenage boy was only present that morning because the family of the friend with whom he had a sleepover insisted that he attend Mass with them. He now proclaimed to his friend, "Dude, your church rocks. I am definitely converting. Definitely. These guys perform every Sunday?"

"Shhh," his friend's mother said.

In fact, mothers all over the church were "shushing" everyone, sons, daughters, husbands, people they didn't even know.

When Mass ended, Stewart attempted to exit as quickly as possible. He was delayed momentarily by Percy's wife, who insisted on a photograph of Stewart and Percy together in church. Stewart placed an arm around Percy's shoulder and smiled perfunctorily.

"Where's your hat?" Percy's wife asked.

Stewart looked at Percy who wore a broad, unaffected smile and a sloppily folded bulletin hat.

"Snap the picture, Meg," Stewart said.

Dee drove on the way home. Stewart kept the palms of his hands pressed against his eyes.

"It was not as bad as you think. The children were the only one's laughing."

Dee glanced over at Stewart, saw that his eyes were still covered and allowed herself a suppressed but brimming grin.

"Dee, Father Hemmler is not a child. He is sixty-one."

"Father Hemmler was not laughing. He was smiling," Dee said. "He may have been praying and was caught up in some kind of spiritual ecstasy."

"He may have blown the speakers out of the back wall of the church with that guffaw of his blasting into his microphone," Stewart said.

When they turned onto their street, Wade came into view. He was standing in the middle of the empty street, smiling broadly and pumping his arms up and down like a giant bird. Stewart had just removed his hands from his eyes.

"Oh, ram him, Dee, just ram him," Stewart pleaded.

Dee stopped the car in front of Wade and rolled down her window. Wade stuck his face into the car. His hair spilled over his forehead, a few strains resting on the top of his eyelashes. The tart, sweet smell of recently consumed alcohol wafted into the car.

"Storks a' flying," Wade said.

"Wade, you're breathing on the children," Stewart said.

Wade smiled his smirk and took his head out of the window.

"Sorry," he said. "It's just that good news is hard to hold in."

"What good news?" Dee asked.

"Charlene's going to have a baby. The doctor called this morning. Called on a Sunday morning. That's what I call service."

Dee's mouth dropped open and a little cry escaped from it. She looked into the rearview mirror.

"You hear that, kids? Y'all are going to have a little cousin."

"Step-cousin," Stewart said.

He put his hands back over his eyes and heard Wade continue to prattle on about the coming events. With Stewart's eyes covered, Wade's voice seemed far away and every possibility and plan he mentioned sounded very remote and unlikely, detached from anyone he knew. He kept his eyes covered as Dee drove up the street towards their driveway. He bounced against the interior of the car door as the Colt surmounted the curb and eased onto the ribbon strips. Dee really was an excellent parker, Stewart thought, with admiration. But the rest, the insufficient funds, the inaccessible uniforms, the paper hats, the Nazi salute, the "storks a' flying" it all sounded like the bad soundtrack of someone else's life. The devil was just having a good day, that's all. He just had to remember that.

Chapter 12

"Did you really think you could get away with machine-gunning the DeLeos' dog?" Mr. Gravier asked, angrily pacing the area behind his desk.

"It wasn't a real—"

"Don't interrupt me," Mr. Gravier said. "Why did you lie to me when I asked you if you were delivering your route armed? Answer me, that!"

"Well, actually—"

"I'm not finished," Mr. Gravier said with increasing annoyance. "I've got a lot to say. I don't know if you realize this but when you're out on your route wearing that uniform, you're not just an employee, you're representing the entire postal service. Indeed, the US government. Indeed, the nation. Do you realize that? Well, do you?"

"Yes, sir."

Mr. Gravier raised his hand.

"Still not finished," he said, dragging each syllable out. "When in the history of our great nation has anyone wearing a uniform and representing the US government ever carried a gun? Tell me that."

Stewart looked at him and wanted to ask, "Are you serious?"

Instead, he glanced out of the office's large windows. He saw a young woman walking towards the post office with two parcels, wrapped in brown paper. She was followed by a toddler who kept his head down, perhaps to guard from the sun's glare, perhaps to search the ground for some overlooked treasure. They both seemed so free and lighthearted to Stewart, although it was likely just his imagination. They, or at least the mom, had responsibilities and worries like everyone else, he supposed. But she was not stuck in this office, enduring this torture. The windows of Mr. Gravier's office were so tinted that a person on the inside could make funny faces at people passing by without ever being detected. The tinting also made the parking lot look as if it were constantly under the threat of rain.

"Are you going to answer me?" Mr. Gravier asked.

"Sir?" Stewart said

"I said . . ." Mr. Gravier said and then actually forgot what he had said. "Were you even listening to me?"

"Yes, I thought—"

"Let me finish, Stewart," Mr. Gravier said. "I think you need to examine your role here at the post office and decide just what your purpose is. Is it to do a job the whole country can be proud of? That our society desperately needs? Or is it to see how far you can bend the rules, how much you can get away with? Do you understand what I am saying?"

"I do," Stewart said. "I would just like—"

Mr. Gravier raised his hand resolutely.

"I think you've said quite enough already. Don't you think God gave us two ears and only one mouth for a reason?"

Stewart nodded his head once.

"Well, do you?" Mr. Gravier asked loudly.

"Yes, Yes," Stewart said.

"All right. Enough said," Mr. Gravier said. "Go case your route. You're inside today. Someone else is going to take route thirteen temporarily. Someone unarmed. Where did you get that machine gun, anyway? Aren't they illegal?"

"It—"

"Never mind. I've heard enough from you already," Mr. Gravier said.

Stewart walked briskly to the office door. When he opened it, the entire post office was silent. People were frozen in various working positions. A row of employees stood before their mail cases, hands containing letters that were not quite inserted into their proper hutches. The freight workers who unloaded bags full of mail at the back of the post office stood with raised stacks suspended between them. The custodian leaned on his push broom expectantly, a pile of dust, candy wrappers, and cigarette butts waiting in still life beneath spindly brown bristles.

Sid stood at the water cooler, a paper cup lifted halfway to his mouth. All eyes were turned toward the office door.

"Coworkers," Stewart said in greeting. He smoothed the front of the airmen's sweater and breathed deeply.

"Stewart," returned the custodian, a rakish youth with earphones and a Walkman.

These words broke the spell of silence and the busy clatter and movement of the office resumed. Stewart walked determinedly toward his case.

"Boy, he was hot," Sid said, coming up from behind him. "I heard every word. Did you say anything at all in your defense?"

Stewart stopped, turned around, looked at him, and said nothing.

Sid held his hands in front of him, palms out.

"Sorry. See you at lunch, Stew," he said.

"I hate this place, Sid," Stewart told him at lunch.

They were seated in Sid's minivan facing the post office. Sid was eating an apple. His door was open, and he had one foot crammed high into the door jamb. The elbow of the hand that held the apple rested against his raised knee.

"Aw, Stew, Gravier didn't mean anything—"

"It's not Gravier. It's not Sir Henri," Stewart said. He looked at the building once more, reading the brushed steel lettering that spelled out its name—New Orleans Post Office, Carrollton Station, New Orleans, Louisiana 70118.

He truly hated the place.

"You know what I pray for every day, Sid? Not wealth or power or even a long life. I pray for the chance to do something on my own. Do you ever feel like you don't even belong here? The floors, the walls, the actual physical space smells of someone else—of the hundreds, the thousands of bodies that occupied the space before you. And look how easily you can be switched from what is supposed to be your space. You're on a route for three years or twenty years or whatever and then, whamo, you're inside or on a totally different route ten miles across town."

Stewart puffed his cheeks and then released a steady stream of heavily burdened air.

"What I wouldn't give to have been Adam," he continued. "He sure screwed things up for the rest of us, but what an opportunity he had. The world probably sparkled it was so new then. He was the first one to work anywhere. He belonged everywhere."

Stewart relished the thought.

"To start fresh. Completely fresh."

Sid bit into the apple, thoughtfully.

"Still, you got to say the pay isn't that bad," he said.

"I'm not talking about pay or a dental plan or vacation time. Can't you see what I'm talking about?" Stewart said.

"Sure, you're talking about starting your own business," Sid said.

"It's bigger than that," Stewart said. "I am talking about being where I belong."

Chapter 13

Well, Charlene was pregnant and that was that.

"Twins," Dee said, taking the salad bowl from the center of the table and putting it next to Charlene. "Plenty of greens," she added. "You're eating for two, well, for three, I guess . . . you know what I mean."

Dee laughed too loudly at her own joke. Wade smirked pleasantly around a section of boudin sausage he had placed in his mouth. Charlene picked timidly at the bowl of salad, fishing out only the greenest leaves of lettuce.

"I don't like tomatoes," she said.

"Twins?" Stewart squeaked.

Stewart looked down at the floor and shook his fist in the direction of hell.

"You just never quit, do you?" he said.

Dee frowned and smiled nervously.

"Stewart?" she said. "Who are you talking to?"

Stewart straightened.

"Huh, uh, nobody, hon, I thought we had a dog. So, twins! How excruciatingly fortunate, remarkably blessed, incredibly propitious. Decided on any names yet?"

Stewart dabbed his mouth and muttered behind his napkin.

"Debit and credit?"

Amy, reaching across the table for a slice of buttered French bread, bumped her elbow against Dee's iced tea.

"Amy, if you want something say, 'May I please have some more?' It's not polite to reach."

Dee touched her hand to her mouth and in a quick kissing motion removed the tea that had spilled from the glass and was trickling down her index finger.

"So, Wade, have you told Stewart the headline news today?" Dee asked.

Wade, who had been reaching across the table himself for another helping of jambalaya with extra sausage stopped in mid motion and leaned back grandly in the chair.

"I got a job today," he announced.

Stewart looked back at the floor and stuck his tongue out squarely in the face of the devil.

"I may see you at work," Wade said. "I'm painting the Pagones' house."

"The big one they lease out?" Stewart asked. "Forty-three, forty-five Cleveland Court. That's terrific."

"A lot of times a job like that can lead to other jobs," Dee said. "People see you working and think, 'Hey, I could use someone to paint my house.'"

"Or do odd jobs," Charlene offered. "My daddy used to make one hundred dollars a week doing odd jobs here and there."

"Well, there you go," Stewart said. "Well done, Wade."

He took a sip from his own tea.

"Twins," he muttered into his glass.

For the next few weeks things went surprisingly well. Stewart could gauge the progress Wade made on the house when he passed it at the beginning of his route each morning. Wade had erected an impressive network of scaffolding on the west side of the house and had begun scraping away the fading peach exterior with which the previous owners had coated the weatherboards. At the end of the first day, he had removed almost a third of the paint of the two-story home, an estimable achievement even allowing for the fact that bottom half of the home was brick. Stewart was stunned, pleased, ecstatic, grateful, and suspicious of the vehemence and thoroughness with which Wade approached the project. Each evening Wade came home exhausted, sunburned, and sweaty. Tiny scales of peach paint covered his hair, face, and arms.

Every new morning, Stewart noted with satisfaction that the scaffolding had been moved forward toward the next section, revealing bare wood with only a light blush remaining from its former salmon covering. In a week, the entire structure had been stripped of its paint and the exposed boards, now whitish-pink and powdery, seemed to be begging for covering.

"Where's your brother?" Mr. Pagones asked one sunny, hopeful morning as Stewart approached the house with his mailbag.

"Step," Stewart said, absently, as he placed mail in the next-door neighbor's box and came off their porch.

Mr. Pagones was standing in the open door of his Buick Skylark. His close-fitted suit, his balding head and his furrowed forehead all seemed to be protesting the exceedingly warm morning sun.

"No, he's not on the steps. This house doesn't even have steps. Don't you think it's about time he got some paint on this bare wood? Some primer even," Mr. Pagones asked. "Bare wood warps when exposed to the elements."

Stewart was now at the Pagones' mailbox. He looked at the tenants' mail, hoping he could find a piece interesting enough to change the subject. He held a yellow postcard-sized advertisement in his hand.

"Oh, lookee here, they're winners of at least one of the following gifts, a Magnavox VCR, a 1989 Ford Escort, a trip for two to Disneyland, or a handsome wooden towel rack. What a lucky current resident."

Mr. Pagones glanced irritably towards the postcard and then back to the house.

"It's been two weeks since the scraping has been completed," Mr. Pagones said. "What could he possibly be waiting for?"

"It's been two weeks since the scrapping has been completed," Stewart said. "What could you possibly be waiting for?"

Wade was listening to Stewart's voice on a portable phone he had won playing a supermarket bingo game. Stewart had happily paid for the installation and subsequent bills for the phone. He considered it money well spent if it succeeded in reducing the number of minutes Wade or Charlene spent in his house using his phone. Keeping certain people out of his home was a top priority of Stewart's. He entertained a standing fantasy of a front door that had customized reactions to individual visitors, dependent upon Stewart's disposition toward them. He envisioned building such a portal, possibly using a garage door opener and a television remote modified for the purpose. The system would be activated by the appearance at the door of any one of several threats with a variety of responses—"modes" as Stewart liked to call them. They were:

> A. Step-relative: This mode bolted the front door and deposited an ashtray on the steps. In the shallow of the ashtray was the stenciled message: "Can this really not wait until dinner?"
>
> B. Girl Scout Cookie Seller: Similar to the step-relative mode, the door was bolted. Only instead of an ashtray, a sheet with a graph showing the relative quantity/price value of Girl Scout cookies compared to store-bought brands was provided to the visitor.
>
> C. Jehovah's Witness Mode: The doors and shutters were bolted. The ground cracked and separated at the witness' feet

until there was a ten-foot moat filled with snapping alligators around the house. A flagpole was erected in the middle of the roof and the Vatican standard was raised. Beneath the standard was a pennant which read, "I've heard. Forget it."

"A house is a lot like a baby," Wade was saying.

"You're never ever supposed to paint one?" Stewart said.

Wade laughed.

"No, bro. You see wood is a living organ, it needs a chance to breathe. You figure for maybe fifteen years that wood was covered with a primer and two thick coats of paint. Its pores are all clogged and whatnot. It's inhumane. What I am doing is giving the wood a chance to clear its pores, like you would a child—sort of an incubation period."

Truth. He was exceedingly intoxicated. Was confusing his metaphors, forgetting where he started off and where he was heading.

"Well, when do you think this incubation period might end, doctor?" Stewart asked.

"Well . . ."

Well, it wasn't before Mr. Pagones's patience had run out and he told Stewart that in his fifty-three years of dealing with people he had never encountered such an astounding level of incompetence, ignorance, and just plain ol' laziness.

"You can tell your brother Wade those exact words," Mr. Pagones said.

"Step," Stewart said.

"Steve. Wade . . . whatever his name is, you tell him what I said," Mr. Pagones said.

The incubation period for Charlene's twins was progressing nicely.

The months leading up to the delivery were ones in which Wade stayed consistently unemployed and nearly constantly in the bottle, squandering the small amount of money he had received for denuding the Pagones' home. He did manage to crawl out of the boozy haze for a certain portion of the day to tramp about the city—uptown, downtown, the Quarter—searching for the winning set of numbers, knowing they were out there somewhere. If not embossed on the next fire hydrant, then scribbled on the next scrap of litter that flew pass his feet, or printed on the front page of the *Times-Picayune*, or embedded in the blue-tiled entryway of certain commercial establishments downtown, or resting on the solar shield of a satellite orbiting far away in silent space.

Lately, he had been concentrating on numbers in the downtown area. He would gather all the numbers he could by 2:30 p.m., make his ticket purchase at the Verti Marte in the French Quarter, then return home via streetcar or bus. He would hand the tickets over to Charlene and then return to the streets. Around 4:30 p.m.

he would call Charlene to remind her to watch the 5:30 p.m. drawing on TV.

"I will," Charlene would say into the receiver. "When are you coming home.?"

He would supply the day's lie. Charlene had taken to the practice of resting her hand against her bloated stomach as she spoke, rubbing it gently, rhythmically, as if to warm its tenants against the cold world they were about to enter, against the vagaries of what was shaping up to be Wade's erratic fatherhood.

"You never talk about the babies," she said into the phone. "I don't even know what you think we should name them."

He said nothing.

"I wish you were home more," she said.

"Yeah, well, as I do," Wade said. "But you know how Stewart's always riding me when I'm there. Sometimes, I think he hates that we even live there. He resents it or something."

"He just wants us to be successful," Charlene said. "That's what Dee says."

"It's easy for him to ride me. He's got it made with that government job of his. What did he say when I asked him to get me on with the mail? He said, I don't 'have the education.' That's the key, getting that high school diploma down, that piece of paper that says . . ."

His voice trailed off. He hated when the phone conversation went like this. Couldn't Charlene just say she had the television on the correct channel now and would see him when she saw him?

When the babies arrived, it was worse. Wade did not take the birth well. He went into the delivery room as he had promised—but he was not much of a comfort. There was more blood than he would ever have imagined, more than he had ever thought possible, really, and he was half-tanked anyway. They had dressed him in some kind of disposable surgeon's scrubs made from heavy paper. His head was covered with a plastic cap and his mouth veiled behind a white surgeon's mask. He was sweating more than Charlene. When the doctor went to hand him one of the babies his eyes expanded with white fear, and he backed away as if it were a venomous snake. Reproached by the eyes of the nurses and attendants, he fell back against a tray of instruments and then bolted out of the room, running desperately through a spinning maze of white walls and silver, wheeled equipment. Green-clad hospital workers passed him in the hallway like phantoms. He finally came out on a fifth-floor fire escape. The city streets swayed and bowed beneath the rusting grate at his feet. He gasped the sweet, octane-heavy air, clanged down the five flights of stairs, flaking rust as he descended. When he finally reached the pavement, he ran off into the diminishing twilight without a thought of where he was going.

After his exit, Dee had to step in as father. She was given the same kind of scrubs and skull cap as Wade. Both were extra baggy because they were made for a man. She looked like a child playing dress up as she padded into the room with the gait of an astronaut and stood before Charlene as she lay on the bed. Except for the shimmering beads of sweat that lined her forehead, Charlene seemed as placid as ever, even disinterested in things happening with and about her.

"Where'd he go?" Charlene asked.

"In the waiting room with Stewart," Dee lied. "Men can't handle these kinds of things—the blood and everything. Didn't you know that?" Dee said.

A male attendant eyed Dee ironically as he replaced Charlene's IV bag.

Charlene gave a meager smile.

"Two boys," she said. "I forgot what we were going to name them."

That made her laugh. She threw her wrist against her forehead.

"Oh, man," she said.

"Darren and David," Dee said. "Although, I am not sure which one is which."

She was looking at the two naked infants lying on thin cotton mats inside plexiglass trays. Their legs and arms clawed and kicked, as if they were riding invisible air bicycles.

"Who do they look like?" Charlene asked.

Dee looked again at the red and highly animated infants. She tried to make an assessment, went to speak, and then shook her head.

"It's hard to say. They look like each other to tell you the truth," Dee said.

Charlene's eyes showed pleased agreement.

"Identical. I'm glad. I know twins who are . . . paternal? They don't look any more alike than Peter and Paul. This is good. I want to dress them alike and all that."

Two nurses were now surrounding the plexiglass trays, busily cleaning the babies. Darren and David protested with greater vigor.

"When's Wade coming back?" Charlene asked.

Dee was spared answering that question by the intrusion of the doctor.

"Mrs. Terry, we're going to be transferring you to a room in just a few minutes. The boys are both fine. Six pounds even—both of them."

He glanced at Dee.

"You don't get that too often."

He turned his attention back to Charlene.

"The nurses just have a few more things to do before we can bring the boys to you. How do you feel?"

"Tired," Charlene said.

The doctor blinked his eyes in empathy, turned his head towards Charlene's feet and nodded. Charlene's bed began to whirl under the power of an unseen orderly.

Stewart did not take the birth well.

"Twins," he sighed two days later when Charlene had returned home. "And did she really need a private room? That's one non-refundable deductible, I'll bet."

"They're sleeping," Dee said.

They had just walked Charlene to the addition and now Dee held a double bed carrier filled with the napping babies. Each was dressed in a woolly, blue body suit. White knitted hats kept their identical noggins warm. On the crest of each was a strip of adhesive tape with the baby's respective names written in block letters.

"Now look as these two. Doesn't their Uncle Stewy think they're just precious?" Dee cooed.

"Step-uncle," Stewart said. "Yes, I am afraid they are very precious, indeed—priceless in fact. "

He reached a hand forward and began digging through the folds of blankets that covered them.

"There's not a price breakdown anywhere here, is there?"

Dee pulled the carrier away from him.

"I am sure you will be able to write them off some kind of a way come tax time," she said crossly.

Stewart walked into the adjacent kitchen to get himself a Coke. On the counter, he placed a tall brown glass Dee had retrieved from the new brand of laundry detergent she was using. He broke an ice cube tray into it and poured the soft drink. He stood vigil as the carbon dioxide dissolved, adding a corresponding drop of soda as the bubbles receded.

"Don't think I won't claim them," Stewart called over the half wall that separated the kitchen from the dining room,

Dee had set the carrier on the dining table. She was looking intently at the faces of the babies, contemplating their placid, porcelain repose.

"I need to put together an itemized account of all the extras of this blessed event—in addition to the private room, I mean," Stewart said.

"What extras?" Dee asked with little interest.

"Well, the circumcisions were good money thrown away," Stewart said. "Literally. And was it really necessary to have all those attendants and hangers-on in the delivery room. It was like a medical convention in there. Do you how much each extra body in that room cost?"

"I have no idea," Dee said, imaging what Darren and David might be dreaming.

"Well, I do," Stewart said. He took a slip of paper out of his breast pocket, surveyed it for a moment and then reached his hand into one of his pants pockets.

"Where is it now?" he mumbled.

Dee was walking toward the back of the house.

"Stewart, keep an eye on the babies, I am going to check on Amy and Timmy."

Stewart nodded and took a sip from his drink.

"No, that's the parking validation I demanded from the front desk," Stewart said to himself and began rummaging through his back pockets.

A low cry from the carrier brought him toward the babies. He held a page before his face and took another sip from his drink as he read. He came to a stop directly in front of the carrier.

"That's," he looked closely at the paper. "That's not even mine," he said and began to crumble the paper.

Each turning, twisting fold of the paper revealed a patch of forehead, a set of tiny fingers and finally the unwavering stare of the two twins. Stewart placed the ball of paper on the table next to the carrier. He extended his right hand forward and shook each of the infant's tiny hands.

"Stewart George," he said. "Glad to meet you. One bit of step-uncle advice that will serve you well—observe your father's every action closely, pay unremitting detail to every one of his moves, schemes, ventures, articulations, and inclinations. And then do the exact opposite."

Chapter 14

The Colt finally died. It had stalled on a busy overpass one afternoon when Stewart was driving home from work. With car horns honking savagely behind him and three miles between the end of his bumper and the beginning of his driveway, Stewart had solemnly sworn that he would trade in the car no matter how insignificant the current problem was or how inexpensive its remedy. As it turned out, the problem was neither insignificant nor inexpensive.

"Your struts are busting fluid," the mechanic said coming out from underneath his car on a creeper.

He squinted up at Stewart. He wore an oily Delco cap and had bunched teeth that came out of his gums in conflicting angles. Stewart always felt that something in the make-up of men who worked on cars for a living—he suspected that it was genetic dishonesty, or possibly the amount of engine grease that found its way onto their faces—gave them a common, indistinct age. The mechanic speaking to him could have been nineteen years old or fifty-eight.

"But what's making the car stall?" Stewart asked.

"Your block's cracked," the boy/man said plainly.

Stewart stared at the mechanic.

"Cracked?" he said.

"Whoever put in that new starter didn't notice how hot your motor was running?"

A moment's silence.

"He may not have noticed that he was on earth," Stewart said. "How much will this cost to repair?"

The mechanic looked at the Colt and then blew a stream of air between his bunched teeth that made his lips flutter like a horse's.

"What year is it?" he asked.

"Are you asking me what the current year is or what year my vehicle was manufactured in?"

The mechanic gave Stewart a blank look.

"Seventy-nine," Stewart said.

"I know a man that needs parts for a '79 Colt," the mechanic said. He looked back at Stewart's face again, squinting.

Stewart sold the car for parts and netted four hundred dollars. This made his ears turn red, but they resumed their natural color with the purchase of a Ford Ranger pickup truck. It was a sporty, short-bed model, sleigh red with silver trim. It was the first item Stewart had bought for himself that contained any sort of frills since the Mr. Coffee he had purchased in 1980, much to the astonishment of family and friends. Besides its beauty, the truck was also durable and rugged, which was one reason he climbed and bucked the oyster shell hills that ran behind the Trader's Lounge, without hesitation.

The oyster shell drive ran some five hundred feet behind the bar and its companion buildings, including the insurance office outside of which Wade had of late taken a tumble and rest. The dust tail that followed Stewart as he drove the stretch of shells overtook him and swept by him when he brought the Ranger to a stop. The dust whipped and swirled around the reposed figure of Wade. His back was resting against the cinderblock wall of one of the older buildings. His head was bowed with his forehead resting on top of his folded arms, which were supported by his knees. The skullcap from the hospital kept his hair in a steamed and sweaty bundle. His green scrubs were now thinned and soiled at the knees. Stewart exited the truck and approached him.

"Father of the Year," Stewart said.

He was near the lake now and the air was briny with a constant breeze.

"He's a sleeper, that one," a voice said behind Stewart.

Stewart exited the truck and approached him. The voice seemed to speak through the light.

"Lots of thrashing about with that one—and cries. Horrible cries in the night. Sounds like he's singing some song, and the only words are them piercing cries. I thought he was a banshee or a screech owl the first night, but no he's only a man, just like me."

Suddenly a figure appeared out of the light, toothless with a bright orange moving blanket draped across his shoulders. His head was covered by a yellow bandanna, worn maid style. Thin strains of dark hair shot out both sides of the bandanna and into the corners of his dark empty mouth.

"Lots of sleep that one, but not much rest," the man said.

"Thank you for that insightful commentary," Stewart said.

The man's mouth opened, and his tongue contracted until it appeared as a quarter-sized piece of pink flesh. A high, gasping laugh escaped him, wracking his entire frame with potent mirth. Stewart eyed him warily.

"Theodore L. Silva's my name," the man said after he had recovered himself. He thrust a sun-darkened and filthy hand toward Stewart which was ignored. "I live over there," he added jerking the thumb of the refused hand behind him. The spot indicated by the thumb was a tree that stood some fifty feet across the shell drive.

"Love what you've done with the place," Stewart said, but his eyes were looking at the branch of another tree—a still immature, but sizable and sturdy live oak that grew close to the building against which Wade rested.

"That will do," Stewart said.

"My friends call me Ted, if I had any," the man said and took to another fit of laughter. He pumped one crooked arm against his sides, as if to squeeze the merriment from him, bagpipe style.

Stewart looked toward Wade.

"You really are going to have to be more careful about who you invite to these garden soirees of yours," he said.

That remark struck another note of humor in the man. He covered his head with his blanket and rocked back and forth like a child under it, laughing uncontrollably. Stewart climbed up to the wheel of the Ranger, breathed in the new car smell for a moment, and then did a tight 180 that brought the rear bumper of the truck just inches from Wade. The tailpipe vibrated menacingly, sending hot carbon dioxide against his face.

"Stewart?" Wade called out groggily. He coughed and waved the fumes from his mouth. Then he dropped back to sleep.

Stewart exited the cab of the truck and positioned himself in the middle of its bed. He lashed the cable from a block and tackle over the tree branch. Once secured, he stepped out of the bed and stood just to the side of Wade. Grimacing from the smell, Stewart ran the end of the cable underneath Wade's arms and clasped it across his chest. He then began to pump the lever of the block and tackle and watched as Wade started to rise from the ground. Ted removed the blanket from his head, stopped laughing and looked in wonder at the green-clad man floating above him. He clapped his hands together at the miraculous sight. When Wade's hanging body was centered over the bed of the truck, Stewart paused and wiped the sweat from his top lip with his hand.

"Going down, Wade. Brace yourself," he said and instantly tripped the trigger of the block.

The released cable blurred through the pulley and Wade went crashing into the bed of the truck.

"Ohhhhh," Wade moaned.

"Sorry, bed liner hasn't arrived yet," Stewart said.

He pulled the cable from the branch, switching it deftly over the ridged bark, gathered the cable and the block and placed them in the narrow cranny behind the cab's front seat. He took off with a jerk and Wade tumbled backwards. His feet sloshed up and over the tailgate and his face was pressed against the bed of the truck. A quarter mile down the road, Stewart pulled into a Texaco station, filled his tank and received a token for a free car wash.

"Ahhh! Hey! What is this?" Wade yelled as foamy pink water sprayed on him and the oversized blue brush bristles of the carwash whirled towards him.

Stewart sat idly in the sealed cab of the truck reading his owner's manual. Twenty minutes later he sat across a picnic table from Wade with a large McDonald's bag between them. It was a sparkling March morning. The sky was chipped ice blue, the sun as genial as ever. Far off in the distance a children's soccer game was in progress.

Nearer to them, a row of swings sent their human pendulums higher and higher.

"Two Quarter Pounders, a large order of fries, and one unreasonably giant Coke," Stewart said reaching into the bag and placing the items before Wade.

"Root beer," Wade corrected.

Stewart allowed a close-lipped, impatient smile.

"Root beer," he said.

He took one regular hamburger for himself and a small drink.

He laid the white bag underneath the food for a place mat. Wade drew long and hard on the root beer's straw. He gasped when he took his mouth away and then rubbed his fingers together curiously.

"I feel sticky," he said.

"That's the wax," Stewart said, biting into his hamburger.

Wade rubbed his cheeks. They shone brightly. He looked at Stewart with just the slightest bit of indignation.

"I thought I deserved a waxing—free with any fill up, by the way—after rescuing you from that maw of hell," Stewart said. "I am pretty certain your hyena of a neighbor would have eventually eaten you after the proper amount of cautious circling."

Wade touched his face again.

"How long was I there?"

"A week," Stewart answered immediately. "How long were you planning to stay?"

Wade shrugged.

"How's Charlene?" he asked.

Stewart waved his hamburger.

"She's okay."

"And the . . .?"

Wade looked in the direction of the swings and fell silent.

"The twins," Stewart said. "Darren and David. They're fine. You think you might drop by and see them before they register to vote?"

Wade looked at Stewart and then back at the swings.

"I've never been so scared to death in my life, man," he said. "There I was just looking down at this baby all slimy and bawling. It looked like an animal to me. Like one of them blind piglets you'll come across when you're out hog hunting. The one whose mama's been shot and they're just wandering alone and blind in the world. I looked down and I seen this little creature pawing the air and I think, 'I got to make this animal into a human.' And not just one, but two of them. And then it all just come down on me then and there, all this terrible knowledge and burden of responsibility. You know what I mean?"

"No," Stewart answered truthfully. He hadn't the slightest idea what Wade meant. The knowledge of responsibility was something he thrived upon, a welcome weight that kept him anchored and secured.

Wade pulled his skull cap off his head and held it against his eyes. His head was alive with a persistent pain.

"I've got to be the worst daddy in the world," he said

and laughed sadly.

"Got my vote," Stewart said, reaching across the table for a handful of his French fries.

Wade took the cap away from his eyes.

"So, what would you do if you were me?" Wade asked.

"Well, there's a profoundly disturbing thought," Stewart said. "But let's not torture the imagination. I will, however, give you some advice. Why don't you come home and try to be the world's best dad? You won't become that, to be sure, but with time, you might achieve some level of halfway decency. They're not animals, by the way. They are beautiful baby boys."

That night, after Wade had come home and made his peace with Charlene and had awkwardly taken the boys into his arms and tucked them into their cribs, he pulled down a quilt that separated the kitchen from the living room, wrapped it around himself and silently moved out of the house.

The streets of the neighborhood, far from the blaring neon revelry of downtown were silent and empty. It was quite cold. Businesses and homes were shuttered, locked, and clamped down against the frigid night. The new moon, hanging low in the western sky, shed its pale grace on the surroundings giving a dappled luminescence to certain surfaces, the waxy leaves of a row of holly, the stucco exterior of a Hibernia branch, the sturdy peaks of home, the gray-white swirl of the concrete streets in various stages of disrepair.

It took him an hour and a half of steady walking before he arrived at this destination—a cloaked, moon-bathed figure lying beneath a tree that grew behind a familiar row of low-slung businesses not far from the lake. The old man's yellow bandana stuck out from beneath the bright orange moving blanket. Wade took the quilt from around his shoulders and laid it gently on top of the orange blanket. When the old man would wake the next morning, he would have no idea from where or how this gift came to him; but he would be grateful for it. He needed to guard himself against the cold and the truth that finally settles upon you after all your daylight dodging. Wade knew that. He was not the only one who cried out in the night.

Chapter 15

Darren and David grew in strength, size, and rascality as they entered toddlerhood.

"Stewart, they are not communists," Dee said after he had alluded to this possibility for the third time that week.

"I wouldn't be so sure," Stewart said. "You see how they're always huddling so close together, making plans. What do you suppose they've got on their minds that is so secretive, anyway?"

Stewart was looking out at the two as they played in the dust beneath one of the backyard trees.

"Maybe they're planning an escape," Timmy said, sourly.

He now spoke with the deep unsureness of early adolescence and seemed to survive solely on sleep and sarcasm. Secretly, Stewart admired his ability at the latter.

"I don't think I like your attitude again, general," Stewart said.

Dee felt her stomach constrict during the silence that followed. Amy, now eleven, and showing every sign of becoming a beautiful teenager, peered around the corner of the easel on which rested a watercolor seascape she was painting. Stewart and Tim, as he liked to be called, had been locking up like this on a fairly regular basis now.

"I'm going to Mark's," Tim said.

"Don't smoke any pot," Stewart countered.

A year ago, Dee had come across a plastic baggy with a sprinkle of powdery brown marijuana in Timmy's sock drawer. He claimed he was keeping it for a friend. Stewart ordered that he flush the substance down the toilet and lose the privilege of seeing his friends for the next eight thousand days. He had served what felt like a good quarter of that sentence before Dee had intervened on his behalf. Now, he looked at Dee, hoping to evoke some additional clemency on her part.

"Just go," Dee silently mouthed to him.

Amy returned to her painting. Amy, effervescent Amy, a joy of joys, beautiful inside and out. Had she ever done anything wrong? Anything? Ever? Tim wondered. He shoved past Dee and out the door.

Charlene suddenly came into Stewart's view as he continued to stare out the window. She was checking on the twins. Her stomach was drooping with the weight of another child, and she held an infant in her arm.

"Going for a world record, are we Wade?" he mumbled.

Two days earlier, Wade had been relieved of his duties at the Crescent City Construction Company. He had held the job for a year and a half—a personal record—but had lost it for showing up drunk one day, not at all the next, and even drunker the following one.

Dee had convinced Stewart to go speak to Wade as the latter sat in one of their backyard metal lawn chairs, mulling over his firing. They were supposed to have a heart to heart. That was what Dee had suggested. She appealed to Stewart to speak to Wade about his burgeoning family, his drinking, his job situation.

"Really talk to him—man to man. Don't just mumble insults and hope he can get the proper direction by reading between the lines," Dee had said.

Stewart mumbled something in reply and walked out the back door.

"Fired for drunkenness! You?" Stewart asked as he came down the back steps. "I won't believe it. Someone must have planted it on you. Think, who is your worst enemy on the site?"

Wade looked up from his sitting position.

"No, it's true, bro," Wade said. "It's okay, though. I guess I was getting tired of working there anyway. It was the same old thing every day, you know what I mean?"

"Not really," Stewart said. "Delivering mail is so filled with variety and wonderment. No two stamps are ever the same."

Wade was now looking up at the sky as if appraising its value.

"I guess the Lord just didn't want me there," Wade said.

"If you are going smite him with a bolt right at this moment, God, kindly let me remove my person out of the strike zone first," Stewart thought.

"I just wish I could hurry up and win that lottery. I haven't been able to get even one digit in the winning series they been calling, lately."

"It just isn't fair that you haven't won it yet," Stewart said. "Someone who has worked as hard as you all his life deserves to be handed twenty million dollars."

"Thirty million," Wade said. "It was up to that this past weekend. But I'm patient. I'm patient."

"If you could manage to take out that ant pile near the fence line in the same strike, Lord," Stewart thought.

Charlene had learned of her most recent pregnancy by using a home testing kit. She completed the test but refused to look at the result. Instead, she sat before the kit for a good half hour with her hands over her mouth and her eyes staring at the bathroom wall. She knew. She knew she was. Tears began brimming in her eyes and then spilled down her cheeks and ran into the gullies formed by the fingers clamped to her mouth. Finally, she moved her hand and looked down at the kit.

She was. By this time, Wade had become quite accustomed to the idea of fatherhood. He gloried in the ability it showed on his part and the instant gravitas it gave him in whatever circle of society he wandered into. She could not bear to have his unbridled joy accompany her first announcement of the news. She hurried instead to Dee with the results.

After she told Dee, she sat at the kitchen table and bit savagely at the tattered nail of her index finger. Three times Dee had started a sentence with a consoling, "Charlene" but had never been able to continue. Charlene lit a cigarette and a finger thick spiral of smoke rose into the pristine air of the room. Dee winced, knowing Stewart would be infuriated by the smell of smoke in the air, which he would easily detect when he returned home some three hours later.

"Charlene," she began a fourth time and paused again.

"I don't mind the children," Charlene said. "It's the hospital. I feel like I'm going to go in there and never come back—every time. Children, I don't mind so much," she reiterated. "They're the only things that don't kill. You watch the news? Everything kills, men especially, but little boys, too, sometimes, and even girls. Everything kills someone or something. Even animals like dolphins that are supposed to be so nice and smarter than dogs. They kill, too."

She was accustomed to having what she said ignored or debunked. She dismissed it herself now with a slight shrug and a long pull from her cigarette. Dee stood up and walked to the sink. She brought back a small ceramic teacup that she kept next to a dish soap dispenser. She emptied its contents on the table between them. From among the confusion of earrings, chains, and several odd sized washers she selected a flat, tarnished medal.

"My mother gave this to me," Dee said. She picked up Charlene's left wrist, the one without a cigarette at the end of it and pressed the medal into her palm.

Charlene took the medal between her thumb and forefinger and eyed it indifferently.

"St. Jude," Dee said. "Patron Saint of hopeless causes. It can't hurt."

"I ain't Catholic," Charlene said. "Does that matter?"

Dee shook her head, "I don't think so."

"Well, thanks," Charlene said.

"Charlene," Dee said. "Did you ever pray to *have* a child?"

Charlene laughed. "Why would I do that? No."

She gave another, genuine and hearty laugh, which was not her custom. It ended with an undignified snort and cough.

"What made you ask that?"

Dee shrugged. "No reason. I was just wondering."

Chapter 16

That night, Dee approached Stewart again about speaking to Wade. Two days later Stewart was standing beside a poster that rested on Amy's easel. At the top of the poster was the heading, "Yearly Growth of World Population."

Across the bottom of the poster were the calendar years, 1984-1989.

A staggered graph line of peaks and valleys made its way across the board which was divided into major headings: "East," "West," and "Developing World."

"Wade, the following is a diagram of the shift and trends in world population during the past five years," Stewart said.

He brandished a pointer.

"As you can see the West showed an annual growth rate of 1.9 percent throughout this period, while the East showed a yearly increase of approximately 1.7 percent. The 'Developing World' had a somewhat larger rate."

He tapped his pointer against the "Developing World" section with its jagged line struggling ever upward. Stewart then removed the poster and replaced it with another. It contained the same graph but with only one thick red line rocketing straight upward and off the board, with no lateral deviation.

"This is you," Stewart said, tapping the line. "It continues on the back."

Dee turned the page of the magazine she was reading with a loud switching sound. She had slipped off her shoes and brought her feet up and under her on the sofa.

"Don't you think it would be better if you could just talk to him in plain language?"

Stewart was examining the first poster graph, holding it at arm's length.

"Do you think I should use a darker shade for the East? Something tyrannical?"

"I think you should listen to me," Dee said.

She had risen from the sofa and now clasped both of her hands on his forearm.

"He doesn't need to be given lectures or shown graphs about global population. He needs someone to talk to him. This is Charlene's fourth child in as many years. The girl cannot hold up under that strain. Tell him that. For all his faults, he does actually care for her."

"I don't know what I can tell him," Stewart said. "You

know how the church feels about . . ." and he lowered his voice to a strained whisper, "B-I-R-T-H C-O-N-T . . ."

Stewart trailed off and frowned, moving his lips silently, questioningly.

"R-O-L," Dee finished.

"Exactly," Stewart said. "Thank you. I am not a great air speller."

"Still, you could talk to him. There actually are other M-E-T-H-O-D-S."

"Methods," Stewart said, and then brightened. "Perhaps, I could write the archbishop and obtain a special dispensation for the use of A-R-T-I-F-I-C-I-A-L C-O-N-T-R-O-L. If there's one thing I can do, it's write a letter. I'll go start on the first draft right this minute."

He walked out of the living room and bounded upstairs. For the time being he had completely forgotten his graph and his presentation, his research on world population, his charting, his shading, and his pointer.

Dee plopped back down on the sofa in disgust.

"You D-O T-H-A-T," she said.

"Finished," Stewart said, coming down the stairs. He ran his tongue luxuriously along the seal of a business envelope. Four days had elapsed since he had begun the first draft.

Dee grimaced at the steam rising from the pot of rice she had just poured into a colander.

"Finished what?" she asked.

"My letter requesting a dispensation," Stewart said.

"Oh, Stewart. What are you going to do with the letter? Nail it to the archbishop's door?"

"No, I am going with a much more effective means, the US Mail. And, unlike *The Ninety-five Theses,* which you so aptly reference, I am including a small contribution—a little lubricant to oil the ol' canonical wheels, if you will."

"Actually, I won't," Dee said. "Please tell me you are not attempting to bribe the archbishop."

"Bribe!" Stewart said. "Don't be ridiculous. Do you think archbishops care about money at all? I don't even mention the contribution, which is a love offering really, in the letter."

The letter (translated from the original Latin):

His Excellency Philip M. Hannan
Archbishop of New Orleans
7887 Walmsley Avenue
New Orleans, LA 70125

Your Excellency:

For the past five years I have, in accordance with the Biblical injunction to love thy stepbrother, supported financially, spiritually and in various other ways one Wade Terry, his wife and his exponentially expanding family. (See colored population chart, Fig. 1).

I am well versed in the church's teaching (Humanae Vitae, et cetera, et cetera) vis-à-vis artificial means of birth control. I attended Catholic grammar school and high school and completed two years at Loyola University. However, since my brother is, on any spiritual barometer, a goat, I felt led to inquire whether, in your holiness's most considered, gracious and beneficent opinion, I could advise him to practice one or more of the less natural means of population control. Containment of my stepbrother's familial explosion would free my funds to aid in the Catholic education of my two saintly foster children and to further support the corporal works of mercy conducted by my nun-like wife.

Your Humble Servant
Stewart George
Grand Knight, Council, 3685

P.S. Enclosed is twenty dollars to help oil the ol' canonical wheels. Please send me a cash receipt.

The response (translated from a shredded piece of archdiocesan stationery):

George Stewart
Grand Knight, Council, 3685
5335 Greenwood Avenue
New Orleans, LA 70124

Dear Mr. Stewart:

Thank you for approaching our office with this very important matter. I suggest that you contact your parish priest at St. Andrew's as he would be in the best position to counsel you on this problem, which is more of a pastoral concern rather than canonical issue. I can, however, tell you that the church's view on artificial contraception is rather settled, and it is highly unlikely and unrealistic that a dispensation could be granted in this instance. Thank you and may God be with you.

Yours in Christ,

Nicholas D'Antonio
Vicar General
Archdiocese of New Orleans

P.S. Thank you for your generous monetary contribution. It has been earmarked for use by the Catholic Relief Services of Greater New Orleans.

"I'm a Catholic in need of relief," Stewart hissed.

He then shredded the piece of stationery methodically, allowing the slices to fall into and around the wastepaper basket next to his desk. He took the cash receipt, folded it neatly, and placed it in his wallet.

That was a week ago. Now he was sitting again with Wade in the backyard, trying again to have a man-to-man, dead-in-the-eye, serious-as-heart-attack, talk with him. He wasn't doing very well. Wade was rattling on again about that ever-loving Yankee lottery—the chances, effort, and opportunities—and anything else that happened to cross his mental range, which wasn't much except that ever-loving Yankee lottery—the chances, effort, and opportunities. Meanwhile, Stewart, whose hard metal chair was now heating up quite nicely in the warm fall afternoon, was slowly and willingly being drawn down into a deep and satisfying slumber.

Chapter 17

Dee remembered the first time she saw him. He was rushing towards her in that steady gait of his with his schoolbooks tucked high under his arm. His jaw was set in a determined manner, his eyes were centered, yet uncertain, his lips pressed white. She stopped in her tracks and stared at him as he passed her. Her friends walked ahead of her, then stopped and watched her watch him. They giggled. Dee blinked and giggled herself.

"Who?" she said.

"Who cares?" said Cynthia Bonano, the leader of Dee's four best friends—the girls with whom she ate lunch, studied with, and practiced next to on the dance team, "He's a junior."

It was Dee's senior year of high school, a year that was supposed to be filled with the pre-packaged, preordained rituals and everlasting memories of her senior ring, her senior yearbook, her senior homecoming, and her senior prom. But after that day, she could think of nothing else but that junior's face. It was a handsome enough face, to her anyway, still deep in the unfulfilled promises of adolescence. But what struck her the most, was the full-grown air he possessed, the full measure of a man already embodied in his growing, wiry frame.

"George Stewart," one of the girls said as they walked towards Cynthia's car a few days later. "He's in my chem class. He's gross, Dee. He always raises his hand and asks the dumbest questions—like theoretical or theological questions. He thinks Mr. Hubbard is a communist."

"It's not healthy to pursue younger men," Cynthia cautioned. "Look what happened to Cher."

She opened her car door and slid the keys across the roof to Dee who fumbled with them and then opened the passenger door.

"He's an altar boy at my church," said one of the girls on another day. "Who is still an altar boy in high school? It's unnatural."

"George?" Dee called to Stewart a week and a half after she had first seen him. He was arranging the books in his locker. On the inside of the locker door was a picture taken from a calendar Stewart had received from the Sacred Heart League. It portrayed a sad-eyed savior, with a thorn-entwined heart, pink and illumined and lying against a pleated tunic, pressed and pure white.

Stewart turned and looked at her, full faced. Dee

watched the set jaw, those steady eyes, and the full measure of the man immediately fall away and be replaced by a schoolboy's blush.

"Yes?" the boy said.

Dee was dressed in her dance team uniform. It had a pleated skirt with pom-pom boots, a sleeveless top, and a large kerchief that laid flat against her back. The kerchief was clasped in the front by a gold cuff in the shape of a cougar's head with gemstone eyes.

"I see you in the hall all the time. I just wanted to meet you."

She thrust her right hand in front of him.

Stewart looked at the hand with consternation. He had never touched, let alone shaken a girl's hand before. Really, he didn't think girls even shook hands. He based this belief on the actions of the only females in his life— his mother, grandmother, and aunts. They did not shake hands. They kissed one another and him on the cheek. He made an imperceptible move toward Dee to do just that and then blushed ever more deeply. Dee dropped her hand to her side and let it brush against the frills of her skirt.

My name is Dee Duplechain," she said.

"Yes," Stewart said.

"Well, it was nice to meet you. I have to run now," Dee said and hurried away.

"You are on the dance team," Stewart called after her.

Dee turned.

"How'd you guess?"

"Dance teams are very useful," Stewart said. "In many ways I think they define a school."

Dee shrugged.

"It's fun."

"You dance on the field at all the games," Stewart said. It was a statement that needed confirmation, not a question.

"Yes, at halftime." Dee said.

"At basketball and baseball games, too?" Stewart asked.

"Well, at the basketball games, yes and baseball, well . . . nobody goes to the baseball games. I mean not the cheerleaders or band or the dance team."

"I wonder why?" he asked.

"I don't know," Dee said and laughed. "It's just always been like that, I guess."

"It's probably for the best," Stewart said.

"Yes," Dee said, "Probably."

"I bet a baseball could kill a cheerleader," Stewart said. "I mean if she were facing the stands and trying to whip the crowd into a frenzy and an errant foul hit her right in the medulla oblongata—whammo, dead."

Dee nodded, "Possibly," she said.

"Would you like me to call you by your first name or your last name?" Stewart said.

Dee bit her lower lip and tilted her head to the side. Maybe this guy was gross.

"My first name would be fine, I think," she said.

"Good. And feel free to do the same with me," Stewart said.

That evening Stewart came to an abrupt stop as he completed his algebra homework in his four-subject spiral notebook.

"Today, I met a girl named Dee Dupelchain. She is a member of the dance team, a defining institution of our high school. She is astonishingly beautiful. I think I may love her," he wrote below a particularly complex formula.

For the remainder of the school year, he and Dee said hello to each other each and every time they passed in the hall—which turned out to be exactly four times a day.

"Hello, Dee," Stewart would say.

"Hi, George," Dee would answer.

It became more of a duty than anything else, Dee thought. Yet neither altered the path they took between classes or sped up or slowed down in the hopes of avoiding these *quater in die* convergences. No other words were exchanged between them and yet Dee often found herself defending him to a group of her friends. But, she was quickly realizing, the fire in her argument came not from an impassioned heart but from a tender conscience that abhorred the deceit and pretense of false friendliness. The initial impact of their first meeting faded quickly as Dee became entrapped in the distractions of her senior year and started dating another senior. It was not until she was a sophomore at the University of New Orleans, and he a freshman across town at Loyola, that they spoke again outside of their daily high school greetings, which had continued until Dee's graduation.

She was sitting cross-legged on the highly glossed floor of one of the campus hallways waiting for a friend to be released from history class. An opened notebook lay on her bare legs from which she was trying to memorize kingdom, phylum, subphylum, class, order, family, genus and species for an upcoming quiz. Stewart was posting leaflets on the bulletin board next to her. She recognized him by his shoes, the same dark loafers he had worn in high school.

"George?" she said to his shoes and then glanced up the length of his pants to his face.

"Hello, Dee," he said.

"Still dancing?"

"No," Dee said, letting a hand fall against the open page of the notebook. "UNO doesn't have a football team. I liked dancing on the field outside, rather than inside, you know?"

"Heck of a baseball team," Stewart said eagerly. "If you can believe what you read in the paper."

Dee paused before she spoke, making certain she had heard him correctly.

"You probably can," Dee said.

Stewart looked thoughtful. He was actually debating it in his mind.

"Yes, probably," he allowed. "They wouldn't lie about something like that, I suppose. Too many witnesses."

He leaned one shoulder against the bulletin board and looked down at Dee's notebook. She didn't write like some girls with big, loopy bubble letters. Her letters crouched low against the blue line of the paper like soldiers ducking under enemy fire. She also wrote far past the red line of the right margin, something that made Stewart uncomfortable.

"You, uh, ever, uh, every—*ever* go to see the baseball games?" Stewart asked.

Dee shook her head.

"I don't like baseball," she said.

"Me neither," Stewart said. "I enjoy reading about it obsessively in the sports section of the newspaper, but the games themselves? No."

Dee creased her forehead.

"What are you stapling to that board?"

Stewart unfurled the stack of leaflets which he had been coiling in his hand while he spoke. He handed one to Dee. It contained a smudged photocopied picture of the Blessed Mother emerging from a cloud above three kneeling children.

"It's a lecture tomorrow night on Fatima at Loyola. Father Engels is going speak on the subject. He's an expert who now lives in Portugal. Would you like to go? To the lecture, I mean, not Portugal. We could go and maybe have some coffee afterwards."

"Coffee?" Dee said.

"Yes," Stewart said. "You're not a Mormon, are you?"

Dee frowned.

"And what if I am?"

Stewart shifted the shoulder that rested against the bulletin board.

"I would say then that we could go out for water or milk or something cool and fruity, a punch of some sort instead maybe since, I am told, Mormons do not drink coffee."

"My mother is a Catholic," Dee answered. "My father says all religions are the same; all that matters is whether a person's heart is good. And I love coffee."

Stewart smiled.

"It's a wonderful beverage."

They attended the lecture the following evening and after they drank coffee at the student union. Stewart asked her out every night for the next three weeks. Then he asked her if "hypothetically" she could ever imagine being married to him. No, he made it sound more remote than that. "If she could ever imagine being married to a man similar to himself in many respects?"

"Purely, 'hypothetically?' Yes," she said and thrust her hand under his arm.

"Is that an unequivocal, hypothetical 'yes' or a qualified hypothetical 'yes?'" Stewart asked.

He knew he was being humorous now and was as shocked as anyone. They were standing at the top of the levee that overlooked the dark waters of Lake Pontchartrain. Along the lake's edge, section after section of immense, barnacled concrete steps jutted out into the water, like some kind of welcoming staircase for invading sea monsters. The dark waters collided and retracted along the steps. Although he had lived in New Orleans all his life, the steps were an abiding mystery to Stewart. He had no idea, for instance, how far they might extend into the water, whether they ended just below the surface or kept going forever downward into the mud-paste bottom of the lake. Although they could not be seen from this distance, he knew that far away, on the other side of the lake, the lights of a small fishing community huddled and shivered in the darkness behind the black bones of broken, splintered piers. He had visited a friend there once. That memory somehow strengthened his resolve. Without warning, he turned to Dee and pressed his closed lips against hers, with more force than she would have liked. She imagined his lips turning white, looking the same way they had looked the first time she had seen him, compressed into two pale strata, as he walked down the hall of their high school. It was the most ill-timed and poorly executed first kiss she had ever received and, yet, when he pulled away, they were both breathless.

"Unequivocally hypothetically is a something of a contradiction, George," Dee whispered.

"Dee, now that we have reached this level of intimacy. I wish you would call me by my first name."

Dee looked into his face, frowning.

"What is your first name?"

Stewart looked hurt.

"All these years and you still don't know?"

"George, I mean . . . what? Who are you?"

"It's Stewart."

Dee covered her mouth to stifle the laugh that was surging within her.

"You mean your name is Stewart George, not George Stewart?"

"Of course," Stewart said.

Dee looked upward and swallowed her laughter again. The thick, star strewn sky above them seemed very close to the top of the levee, like a dark warm comforter being offered against the chill of the night.

"Is there anything wrong with that?" Stewart asked.

"Not a thing!" she said.

"Not a thing," she thought.

Hypothetically, she reasoned that Dee Duplechain-George sounded a lot better than Dee Duplechain-Stewart.

Chapter 18

In the fall they lost Timmy and Amy. The Orleans Parish Family Court sent Dee and Stewart a letter with the date and time on which they were to bring the children to the downtown courthouse for reunification with a father who had suddenly surfaced. Edward Shevard was his name. He was a recently retired petty officer in the United States Navy. His intention was to bring the kids back home to live with him in California.

Stewart read the court's letter—he called it a summons—out loud, holding the page above the lamp shade. He folded the letter and placed it in the small drawer of their nightstand. It was the second time, at Dee's request, he had read the letter. He turned out the light and climbed into bed next to her. She was sitting up with her back resting against the headboard.

"No tears," Stewart said in the darkness. "We knew

when we got into this that there would be a first day and a last day. We had them for more years than we thought we would. Besides, who's to say they won't be better off—although California does seem a bit like hell to me."

The following month they were in the parking lot of the courthouse transferring the children's belongings from Stewart's pickup truck to Edward Shevard's van. The van was an early seventies model painted in what appeared to be a homemade brown. Its tires were slightly larger than standard. Its thin back bumper was filled with Navy bumper stickers. To Edward Shevard's credit he did not have one that read, "Sailors have more fun."

"A van—figures," Stewart said as he and Dee descended the courtroom steps overlooking the parking lot. "I was just glad he wore shoes."

Dee side-eyed him.

Minutes before, the judge had admonished/admired this Edward Shevard, who looked as if he had never gone without shoes once in his entire life. Dee was struck by how angular a man he was, as if the military had long ago flushed out any looseness he may have once possessed, slicing off jaw, shoulders, and elbows at right angles. The children only remotely resembled him, and even then not in ways identifiable in a photograph or close study, but more in manner and movement. He seemed lost in the fitted, short-sleeve polo and gray slacks he wore to the hearing. He was the kind of man who needed a uniform.

"I understand, Mr. Shevard, that you recently retired

from the Navy," the judge said. "I thank you for your service to this nation and I congratulate you for completing the inpatient treatment program this court had ordered."

"Thank you, ma'am . . . Your Honor," Edward answered in a polished Texas accent.

"Despite your long military service, it would appear, sir, that you have another tour of duty to complete. Perhaps your toughest assignment yet—raising your two children. Children who, I don't have to remind you, lost their mother at very young ages."

"Yes, ma'am . . . Your Honor," Edward repeated.

Once in the parking lot, Stewart had begun handing boxes to Edward who received them in silence and marched with them to the van's open rear doors. The bed of the truck was emptied quickly. Stewart took the last two boxes himself. When he went to set them down in the back of the van, he was surprised to find Tim squatting on one knee and inspecting a wooden case filled with compact discs. A flimsy set of earpieces— orange, quarter-size sponges—were fastened to his ears. Stewart could hear rock music emanating from them.

"That's a good way to blow out both your drums," Stewart said, pointing to the plugs.

Tim gave him an empty look and returned to inspecting the discs.

"I read that in a magazine," Stewart said, defensively. "Nothing against the rock. It's just that high intensity so close to your tympanic membrane can cause permanent damage."

"A lot of things cause permanent damage," Tim said.

"He speaks," Stewart exclaimed. He looked to the courthouse and pretended to call in a loud voice, "Could we get a stenographer here?" He looked back at Tim. "The baby just said his first words."

Tim rearranged the discs back into the shallow grooves of the case, quickly.

"I don't like you. Have I ever told you that?" he said.

"You're a selfish ingrate. I've told you that, haven't I?" Stewart said.

Tim put the wooden case down and threw a pulled punch towards him. Stewart flinched, his feet scraping against the asphalt of the parking lot. Tim grinned with satisfaction at the reaction. Edward suddenly came into view.

Stewart cleared his throat.

"You take care now, Champ," he said and thrust an open hand forward.

"Yeah! Hey, it's been great. Thanks for everything. I'll send you a postcard when we get there," Tim said, releasing the hold of his fist and pumping Stewart's hand.

"Swell kid," Stewart said to Edward. He looked back at Tim and pointed to the V-neck of his shirt. "Is that a little mustard you've got there, Champ?"

"Where?" he asked, looking downward.

Stewart pointed to the shirt and then brought his finger up, flicking the tip of Tim's nose, hard. Tim frowned. Stewart laughed and looked at Edward.

"Little game he likes to play with the old man. He got me six times yesterday."

Edward was still holding two boxes of belongings and had a rubber Bud Light key ring stuck between his teeth. He nodded and smiled with his eyes.

"Wahn hoo drive?" he asked Tim and the keys dropped to the floor of the van. Tim snatched them up.

"Cool."

"He's not really licensed or permitted, yet . . ." Stewart said, but then realized both father and son had left.

Stewart moved from the back of the van and walked next to Dee in the parking lot. Amy got out of the van and ran to him. She put her arms around his waist and laid her head against his chest. Stewart placed one hand on top of her head, felt the cool scar of her part and the hard plastic of her bright hair loop.

"Okay, sweetheart," he said, quietly.

"I'll write to you every day," Amy said, her head still pressed against him.

"Okay, sweetheart," he whispered.

She pulled away, hugged Dee and then climbed into the back of the van.

Edward stood before them.

"I will be forever grateful for the schooling, shelter, and love you have provided for my two children. I know Timmy and Amy will miss you both very much and, like me, shall never forget you," he said.

These were words he had written in a letter he wanted to send to them but had been unable to do so when the court declined to provide him with the Georges' address.

"I guess you must figure I've got my nerve only showing up after they're halfway grown, raised," Edward said. "In truth, I can't ever hope to be the kind of father those kids deserve; the kind of father I would like to have been."

He sniffed softly, ruefully.

"But nobody could be the father I wanted to be. Ha, I just..." he flushed, stammered, and showed weak eyes to Dee.

"He likes to be called 'Tim' now," Dee said.

"That's right," Edward said. "Amy told me that. It's just difficult to get used to. When I knew him ... I mean, he just still seems like Timmy to me."

"Me too," Dee said.

The van's engine roared to life as Tim inexpertly started it. He sat high in the driver's seat, craning his neck to get a good view of the parking lot behind him.

"It's clear," Stewart called to him.

Edward, who was now in the passenger's seat waved to them.

The van jolted and sputtered as it crept backwards.

"I'd have a mechanic check that out," Stewart said. "I lost a Colt like that."

Edward raised his hand again and smiled. Dee grabbed Stewart's arm and brought him close to her before he started giving highway directions. The van pulled away and drove haltingly out of the parking lot, letting out clouds of whitish-blue smoke.

Chapter 19

When they returned home, Dee was shocked to see the physical difference the children's absence made. There were these great, awful, empty spaces everywhere she looked now, obnoxious bright squares on the wall where Amy's paintings had hung. The floor of Tim's closet shone new, relieved of the burden of his clutter. The house appeared dizzyingly neat and ordered. When Dee inspected the rooms after their departure, she drew herself close, with her arms folded across her, as if a sudden chill had settled in the house.

The arrival of Wade and Charlene and their kids for dinner did little to fill the emptiness. Wade was full of questions about Tim and Amy's future in California and their father's Navy experience.

"I've often thought I'd like to join one of the armed forces," Wade said.

"Why don't you?" Stewart asked. They were the first words he had spoken throughout dinner.

"Bum back," Wade said. He opened his mouth and let steam escape from an oversized spoonful of red beans and rice he had heaped into his mouth.

"Wade hurt his back on his friend's three-wheeler," Charlene explained. "He had to wear a brace and all."

"Ah," Stewart said. "A nation mourns the loss of her bravest son."

Stewart was the first to finish eating. He retreated purposefully upstairs and returned with a legal pad and pen.

"We have a little business to discuss here, neighbors," Stewart began.

He stopped and eyed Wade.

"If you had a chair that nice in your home, would you put your shoed feet on it?" he asked. "A purely rhetorical question. Please don't devote much energy to answering it."

Wade removed his feet from the dining chair.

Stewart continued.

"We seem to have a pest problem. I found these shavings from our banana tree."

Stewart took a small, clear sandwich baggie from his pocket and set it on the table.

"The *new-tra?*" Wade asked, immediately.

"If that utterance refers to the aquatic rodent *Myocastor coypus* whose fur is called 'nutria,' a word consisting of three vowels, then you are right on the money. We shall have to burst open a keg this evening to celebrate your erudition."

Wade grinned, cupped his hands and raised them above his head.

Charlene shivered.

"They're gross. They look like big wet rats with orange teeth."

Dee crinkled her nose at the description.

"They have those in New Orleans?" Dee asked. "In the city?"

"A few in city hall," Stewart said. "But besides its physical drawbacks, the creature is a pest that destroys everything in its sight, a public nuisance and noisome beast that must be dealt with. Any suggestions?"

Charlene shifted a baby from one knee to another and brushed a strain of hair from her eyes.

"We could scare it away," she said.

"How about calling the SPCA?" Dee said.

Stewart scribbled a shorthand version of each suggestion in a notebook he was holding.

"Why don't we leave it alone?" Wade asked.

"Mr. Complacency votes for inaction," Stewart said, making a notation in the pad.

"I'm serious," Wade said. "I think they are kind of cool looking. I say, let it be."

"Now, he quotes a Beatle and asks me to take him seriously," Stewart said. "I'm not going to 'let it be,' Ringo, because this is not Audubon Zoo. This is my, our, we—a beautiful yard with a beautiful home on it and I intend to maintain some standards."

One of the twins took a plastic hammer and whacked Stewart on the knee.

"Wade," Stewart said, looking at the boy and then at him.

"Come here, Darren," Wade said and scooped the boy into his arms.

Stewart was about to speak when David came by and stomped his foot, menacingly, on Stewart's ankle.

"Ahhh," Stewart yelled. "Someone call the cops."

"David," Dee called, and the boy went to her immediately.

Stewart pointed to the baby on Charlene's lap.

"Does he have any attack planned or may I proceed?"

The baby looked at Stewart impassively and then issued a loud burp.

The twins broke into hysterical laughter. The baby stuck his hands in his mouth and gave a toothless grin.

"Dwight!" Charlene said and pumped the knee he was sitting on up and down. She looked ready to burst with her latest pregnancy.

"My suggestion," Stewart said, "is to build a trap in the backyard."

He held the legal pad in front of them. Beneath their list of suggestions was a rectangular cube he had drawn with his pen. Each side of the cube had its length written above it.

"Being a creature of habit, we could probably accurately and quickly ascertain the pattern this beast takes on its nightly forays," Stewart said. "Now if we were to intersect that pattern with a subterranean trap, the sketch of which

I have here, I think we could solve our problem."

"What are we going to do once we get the thing in the trap?" Wade asked.

"Good point," Stewart allowed. "I suggest bagging it and removing it to the nearest wooded area, preferably across state lines, to join its fellow furry friends."

"Or we could call the SPCA," Charlene said.

"Or the SPCA," Stewart said.

That night Stewart sat at his desk, hunched over his plans for the trap. He drew an elaborate sketch of the proposed device complete with an unsuspecting nutria snooping towards the mouth of the hole in which he planned to insert the cage. He sketched a topographical view of the backyard with all the likely routes the animal would take as it foraged. He made a list of habitats, within a one-hundred-mile radius, suitable for relocation of the animal. He copied the phone numbers of the SPCA, pest control, Audubon Zoo, and several animal shelters onto his legal pad. He worked late into the night, even though he had to rise early the next morning for work.

Dee watched him from bed as he laid out his plans so carefully. No tears, she thought. Yes, that was Stewart's way. Just busy yourself so you keep well ahead of your emotions. Trap a nutria. Add another mode to your imaginary front door opener. Build a birdhouse or an addition. See if you can make an anti-crying machine out of some spare washers and copper wire. Find an epoxy or an adapter kit that can fix a broken heart.

Chapter 20

Charlene looked at the varnished cross that stood on the nightstand next to their bed. She had taken a string of yarn and run it through the eyelet of the St. Jude's medal Dee had given her. She then tied the string around the upright beam of the six-inch cross so that the medal hung near where the Savior's feet would have been crossed and nailed. Contemplating the small shrine, she took a long drag from her cigarette and rested her hand on the shelf of her belly. She turned to the sound of an opening door. Wade entered, muddied from his shoes to just above his knees.

"What happened?" Charlene asked.

"Stewart's trap," Wade answered. "I thought he only had one of them things. "

Charlene looked back at the cross.

"He said he was putting out one at each of the nutria's main trails," she said.

"I'm going to start following that *new-tra* around. He's the only one safe in the backyard," Wade said.

So far Dee, a neighborhood dog, Darren, and the meter reader had all fallen into one of Stewart's traps. Wade had been trapped twice now.

"Everything's packed?" Wade asked.

"I reckon," Charlene said, looking around at the cardboard boxes that rested on the floor and the mattress.

Wade walked toward the boxes as if he were going to pick one up, but he only slid it out of the way and knelt on the bed behind where Charlene was sitting. He reached into the pocket of his pants and brought out a slender ladies' wristwatch.

"You're getting mud on the she—"

Charlene stopped and brought a hand to her mouth. The gold watch dangled before her eyes.

"Wade . . ."

"Never mind saying 'Wade, we can't afford it.' The only thing you can't afford is what you don't buy," Wade said.

She took the watch and laid it against the fingers of one hand.

"It's real pretty," she said. "Where'd you get it?"

"From a jeweler friend of mine," Wade said. "Nothing down. I told him I'd pay him when we get settled in Mississippi."

Charlene slipped the band around her wrist and held it out in front of her.

"It's real pretty," she said.

She picked up the cigarette she had placed in the ash tray and took another drag from it.

"You know, Daddy said if you are going to work with him there'd be no booze," Charlene said.

"Have I had a drink today?" Wade asked.

"I'm talking about tomorrow, and the next day, and forever," Charlene said. "Daddy just started working for this company himself and he says if you mess up after he recommended you, he'll bust you up for sure. Maybe ya'll can have a drink or two when you come off the boat on the weekends. But Daddy says no drinking on or before the job. Them's the boat rules too."

"I know," Wade said. "When I win the lottery, I'm going to make people listen to my advice and I'm going to repeat myself like your old man does."

"He ain't old," Charlene said and snuffed her cigarette in the ashtray.

Wade moved one of the boxes from the bed to the floor and sprawled across the mattress.

"Dee said she'd have supper ready soon since we're going to get an early start tomorrow morning," Wade said to the unfinished ceiling above him.

The partition quilts had been taken down and the addition seemed much smaller now. The boxes with the rest of their belongings were stacked in the bed of Stewart's Ranger and covered with a blue tarp.

"I'm going to miss them," Charlene said.

"Me too," Wade said.

Stewart's smiling visage eclipsed the sphere of the LP as he walked towards the turntable that was sunk into his console stereo. Once the arm had been lowered to the spinning vinyl, the snappy notes of Glenn Miller's "In the Mood" broke out over the stereo's speakers.

Stewart spread his hands before his cheery face and began waxing the air in time with the music. He backed away from the stereo, hopping on one foot with the other balanced in the air. He backed into the kitchen in this stance. Dee was slicing carrots into a pot.

"Really, Stewart," she said, but could not be heard above the music. Stewart hopped by and popped a few carrot slices into his mouth.

"Fresh. Good," he shouted. "Nothing but the best for their last meal."

He had the index fingers of both hands extended above his head and was pumping his arms up and down vigorously. The tail of his blue postal uniform shirt hung out—a great swaying fan over his buttocks. *Glen Miller's Greatest Hits* was the only LP he owned besides a sleep-learning recording entitled, *Money,* and a collection of *Best Loved War Songs.* His exuberance for the return of the addition dwellers to the Magnolia State knew no bounds. He had even volunteered to drive Wade and Charlene back to Mississippi himself. Darren, David, and Dwight had left earlier in the week with their grandparents. Dee packed sandwiches for the trip.

"Why are you going this way?" she asked the next morning as Stewart turned left out of their driveway and pulled onto a side street.

"You can get to the interstate this way," Stewart said.

"It's longer," Dee answered.

True. But Stewart was hoping to take such a circuitous route, using every side street and incidental track possible, so as to confuse any future return of Wade and Charlene to the 504-area code. He received with equanimity Dee's numerous redirections, remonstrances, and exasperations as they trekked farther and farther from the most obvious and direct path to the interstate. But it was he who collapsed against the steering wheel when they finally entered the last stretch of city road before the interstate ramp. A row of metal barricades barred entry to the road in front of him and stretched for blocks in both directions. People lined both sides of the avenue, four deep, waiting for the parade to begin.

"Minerva," Stewart said.

"I thought it was this evening," Dee said.

"That's what the paper said," Charlene said. "But then it said they had to move it up to the daytime because there's supposed to be lightning and all that tonight."

"There's going to be a parade, today?" Wade asked, brightly.

Stewart opened his door and kicked one leg out. Several cars were stacked behind him, the passengers disembarking with colorful clothes, coolers, and smiles. All around him people were threading through the line of cars and positioning themselves against the barricade. There was a long blast from the horn of a huge truck and then the swirling confusion of police sirens leading the parade.

"I've never been to Mardi Gras in New Orleans. I'm going. Come on y'all," Wade said.

Wade hopped out of the truck, trotted to the barricade, and began waving his arms over his head.

Dee shrugged.

"Since we're here . . ." she said and leaned against Stewart. He grunted and stumbled, dishearteningly, out of the truck.

"Minerva, the goddess of inconvenience," he said.

Charlene slid across the seat, warily. When they came to the barricade, a local high school band was passing by straight and solemn faced, the drummers the only ones making a sound. A sharp wind, colder than normal for this time of year, blew down the boulevard.

"Hey, throw me something," Wade yelled to each player, waving his arms. "Throw me something!"

"They're not going to toss you their instruments," Stewart told him. "Wait until the floats come by. "

A brightly colored van with "WBAY-FM" painted in dreamy bubble letters on its sides came by blasting the Top Forty. A dull-eyed youth with a stylish crew cut, torn jeans, and a sleeveless T-shirt was tossing glowstick necklaces into the crowd.

"One of the more scurrilous stations," Stewart announced to the group.

Dee and Charlene covered their mouths and pointed to Stewart's head.

"You caught something, brother," Wade said.

One of the glowstick necklaces the boy tossed had landed on Stewart's head, laying on his dark crown like a fallen halo.

"Huh?" Stewart said, but the question was lost by a sudden burst of live music. A blue suited and plumed row of marchers passed by them. The players blew furiously on their horns, as if trying to catch up with the tune that was too quickly escaping their instruments. The crowd broke out in cheers. The band was followed by a group of festively clad, highly studded cowboys on horses. Some of the horses appeared on the brink of panic, trotting sideways and wild-eyed toward the edge of the crowd, defecating with abandon.

The king and queen floats passed next and departed quickly, the monarchs waving their scepters over the crowd. Now the throng of revelers began to press forward, as the first throwing floats came shaking up the street. A field of arms stretched into the air and the shrieks and pleas became deafening.

"Hey! Hey!" Dee called, hopping on her toes. "Come on, Stewart," she said, elbowing him.

Stewart raised both arms listlessly.

"Shower me with trinkets," he said, dryly.

The first float was just inches from the barricade in front of them. It lurched to make the sharp turn onto the intersecting street. The band behind the float came to a complete standstill and after a sharp whistle from the director struck up "Mardi Gras Mambo." People were pressing at Stewart's back. A few kids stood in front of the float, pleading with the operator of the farm tractor pulling it to depart with some of the long white beads that hung around his neck. The driver laughed through his black mustache, shook his head, and then ignored them.

The krewe members on the float began throwing steadily to the crowd. To Stewart's right, a young teen was walking on the narrow board of a section of scaffolding someone had erected. The board dipped and warped under his weight. When he was even with one of the krewe members he leaned against the side of the float for balance and then reached over the lip of the structure, near the thrower's waist. When he pulled his hand back it was clutching a large plastic bag filled with coiled white beads. He held the bag before the crowd, who cheered wildly. The aggrieved krewe member frowned behind his mask and produced a long cane spear with orange feathers and a plastic tip. This he brought down smartly on the youth's head. The float suddenly jerked forward and rolled past and was greeted by another wave of revelers.

"Those long beads are so pretty," Dee said to Stewart. Her face was against the back of a stranger.

Stewart turned to see where Wade and Charlene were, as a second float came up quickly to the barricade. This one sported a huge papier-mâché bust of Ben Franklin holding a tablecloth size copy of the Constitution, the fingers of his free hand thrust forward as if in a moment of epiphany. Doubloons, plastic cups, and rubber balls rained down on the crowd. Charlene was near the back of the crowd, scrambling with her bloated belly for the tiny rubber balls that bounced high and crazily on the pavement before her. Wade was near her with a pair of frilly panties a krewe member had tossed secured to his head. He held the cane spear with which the boy had been crowned in his right hand.

Stewart waved him forward.

"Long beads," he shouted above the music of another passing band.

Wade squeezed through the crowd and came beside Stewart.

"Pretty, ain't they?" he said.

Stewart took Wade's spear and held it over his head as the next float passed. This one depicted the Louisiana Purchase with a Thomas Jefferson who bore a suspicious resemblance to Burt Lancaster. Beads, stuffed toys, and more doubloons rained past the plastic tip of the spear. Just as the float was pulling away a krewe member took a pair of green panties and attached them to the blade of the spear. Stewart took the spear down and pointed it in disgust towards Wade.

"Add that to your collection," he said.

Wade took the panties, grinned foolishly, and pulled them over the pair already on his head.

Another float was passing. Stewart raised the spear and shouted:

"Long beads. Long beads."

Again, trinkets flew past the elevated spear. But this time, a krewe member leaned over the edge of the float and stuck a clear empty plastic bag on its point. Stewart pulled the spear down and examined the bag.

"Tell me people don't wear these under their clothes and make my life worth living," he said to Wade.

"No, brother, that's an empty bag. They keep the long beads in there. We're getting close," Wade said.

Dee leaned over to Stewart. Her face was still pressed against the stranger's back.

"Look what I caught," she said and opened a little bamboo and paper fan with a Japanese print on it. She fluttered her eyes behind the fan. As Stewart looked on, a clump of short purple beads thrown from the float slammed hard against his face, raising a welt.

"Fine," Stewart said, rubbing the inflamed spot on his cheek.

On the next float, Stewart made direct eye contact with a masker and thrust his spear towards him.

"Come on. Long beads. Long beads. We're tourists from Omaha," he called.

The masker nodded, reached below him, and brought

forth three long strands. He looped them with care over the spear. As Stewart brought the spear down, a hand reached, grabbed the beads, and pulled them off the spear. Stewart pulled the empty spear back and banged its end against the pavement.

"Thieves," he shouted to the crowd.

Another set of long beads came spiraling towards him. He reached to grasp them, but they were intercepted by two hands, one black and one white, which wrenched them apart.

"That's *it*," Stewart said. "Wade, let me get on your shoulders."

"Huh?" Wade asked.

"Come on. It's the only way."

Wade shrugged.

"All right," he said and turned his back. "Get on."

"I'm not a gymnast," Stewart said. "You have to squat down."

Wade squatted down on the ground and Stewart straddled his shoulders.

"Okay lift up," Stewart said. "Slowly. Come on. Lift up."

"I am lifting up," Wade said. "How much do you weigh?"

Stewart scratched his head.

"Many grams."

He climbed off Wade's shoulders.

"Here, I'll lift you," he said.

Stewart bent down, grunted, and suddenly Wade was lifted above the crowd, clapping his hands toward the approaching floats.

Dee called to Charlene and pointed at Wade.

"Hey, up there!" Charlene called.

Stewart swiveled Wade around and then moved closer to the barricade. The maskers filled both of Wade's hands immediately. Doubloons fell over him and rang against the street.

"Long beads," Stewart called. "Never mind the coins."

At last, a masker threw two waist-length silver beads directly into Wade's hands. Wade lowered them before Stewart's eyes.

"How about them brother?" he asked.

A surge in the crowd pushed Stewart forward and, if not for the barricade, he would have toppled to the ground. Wade, oblivious to the danger, stuck two fingers in his mouth and whistled shrilly. More throws were heaped into his hands. As he caught the throws, Wade would toss them back to Charlene. Soon a dozen multi-color beads hung down the length of both her arms and were stacked about her neck.

"Vertebrae break!" Stewart announced. He squatted down and deposited Wade onto the ground. Before he could rise again, Dee pushed through the crowd and bounded up on his shoulders. Stewart moaned and brought her up above the crowd.

"Roses," Dee yelled. She pointed to Charlene at the back of the crowd. "Roses for the pregnant lady."

Several of the maskers hunched their shoulders and

showed their palms.

"Come on. Roses for the mother-to-be," Dee yelled to the next float.

One masker reached into a box, took two long-stem silk roses out and looked coyly at Dee.

"It's not for me. It's for the pregnant lady," Dee yelled.

The man weighed the possibility. Looked at Dee and then at Charlene.

"Come on that could be your baby," Dee said.

"Dee!" Charlene yelled.

Dee covered her mouth. The crowd around them laughed and hooted.

"I didn't mean—" she gasped. "Y'all!"

The masker threw his head back and laughed. Then he tossed the two roses to Dee and was reaching in another for another when the float jerked away.

Before long, Dee had the two roses stuck behind each ear and was yelling, "Come on, how about some stuffed animals for the new baby? Where are you people's morals?"

"Dee, I've shrunk," Stewart said finally.

He lowered her to the pavement and stood up. A burning pain ran up his spine and branched off into his shoulders. A fire truck came into view, followed by a flatbed truck filled with parish prisoners who were charged with cleaning up the debris produced by the parade. The crowd in the street began to move beyond the barricade, some following the last floats down the road but most heading home. Stewart and the others returned to the Ranger and sat in its cab, waiting for the line of cars to begin moving. The streets were strewn with paper, cans, plastic bags, and beads that had never been caught. The strong odor of horse manure hung close in the air.

Dee and Charlene separated the loot between them.

"What was our final take?" Wade asked.

"Six roses, four cups, fifteen doubloons, many regular beads, twelve long beads—"

"Two panties," Wade interjected.

"Right. And one broken spear," Dee said, holding the spear in front of her. It was cracked and splintered half its length.

"It served us well," Stewart said.

Dee drove the Ranger on the way back from Mississippi that evening while Stewart leaned against the passenger door, trying, unsuccessfully, to relieve the strain on his back.

"I need an aspirin the size of a frisbee. Do they make them that big?" Stewart asked.

"It really hurts, huh?" Dee asked, sympathetically.

"Take the worst pain you've ever experienced, multiply it ten thousand times, concentrate it in one small area of your body, and then have someone strike you many times with a broomstick and you'll have an inkling," Stewart said.

Then he moaned.

"You had fun, though," Dee said.

"Huh?"

"Today. You had a great time."

Stewart shifted his weight again slightly, painfully.

"Yeah, great time," he said.

"No, really. We had a great time, all of us. You had a good time. Admit it," Dee said.

"Okay. I had a good time," Stewart said. "Would you like me to sign an affidavit of some sort?"

"No, I just want you to realize that you do know how to have a good time with your family. It's important to learn that."

Stewart moaned his assent.

Chapter 21

Wade sat with his legs tucked beneath him and his back resting against an outside corner of the tugboat's cabin. An irregular block of pale light fell from the cabin's window and illuminated the tip of his right boot and the top of one knee. All around him was complete darkness. The sky above him was starless with no moon. The water below him was the color of oil and lapped against the hull of the boat with an almost sickening thrust and draw. Inside the cabin four men, including his father-in-law, sat around a peeling, vinyl-topped table playing cards. Wade had not been invited to play. His father-in-law had decided to level with the captain of the tug. In the presence of the other crew members, he had told him that Wade was an alcoholic, incapable of holding down a job, and chronically lazy—that he lacked discipline and resolve and wanted something for nothing.

The words were taken to heart by the captain and the other crew members and likely had the opposite effect Charlene's dad had predicted. Quite from turning them against Wade, he became their special project. No vice was to be spoken of or performed in his presence. The crewmen resolved to set themselves to their duties with extra energy and without complaint. By silent assent they conspired to serve as living examples of the value of an honest day's work with a sober, unadulterated mind. Lottery dreams were smoke. This difficult and dangerous work upon this boat, this grip of line and wire, the coaxing of ratchets and winches, breaths of diesel, threat of sun, caprice of wind and wave was the way to scratch and struggle out a living—better to endure Adam's curse of labor than beg pennies from heaven. A few crewmen even went so far as to eliminate profanity when in Wade's presence or to give into it only in the most righteous tones, prompted by exasperation that they could not fit more work into a single day.

The first day on the water, the tug was assigned an inland route, steaming two giant barges filled with four towering heaps of dredged clam shells upriver. The gray-white shells still held the odor of their long dead inhabitants and the stench of the sea. They attracted swarms of buzzing green flies and squawking gulls. Wade was sent to the galley of the boat where he was assigned the task of removing years of accumulated grease from behind an ancient, white stove.

"Get it off the walls, too," the captain ordered. "I want all that area behind there cleaned, sparkling."

The galley, like every other place on the tug, was cramped and noisy. Its walls vibrated from the pounding of the three-thousand-horsepower engine below. Wade took the trowel he had been given and began lifting the amber, congealed grease off the floor at the rear of the stove and emptying it into a plastic bucket. By noon his shoulders were stitched with pain from the awkward, repetitive movement needed to reach the grease behind the stove. But the area was free of grease, and he had begun scrubbing flecks of grease off the wall when the captain appeared again.

"That's good enough," he said without satisfaction. "Your father-in-law tells me you're a painter."

"Yeah, well," Wade said rubbing one shoulder and grimacing.

"Outside of the cabin needs repainting," the captain.

He handed him a paint scraper no wider than a ruler and, magnanimously, told him that he could begin on the side of the boat's cabin that was away from the sun. The metal sung against his scraping, and he had smoothed the entire starboard side of the structure before the sun had worked its way to his side in an angry burst that broke against the metal, like wave to rock. At sundown there had been a meal at a table where the conversation was antiseptic and muted.

"Cards," the captain announced at the end of the meal. "Dishes, Wade."

Wade cleared away the dishes from the table, washed, and stacked them. When he turned from the sink, the bodies of his shipmates seemed to have enlarged and the table, which moments before had easily accommodated six men, now seem to allow for no more than five. Wade had then taken his seat outside the cabin. Another crew member was standing watch, so he had little to do. Laughter and the hiss of beer cans opening wafted through an open window above his head. He sat placidly, letting his low breathing fall in with the rhythm of the lapping water. Hours later a foot nudged him awake.

"Good way to fall overboard," a voice said.

It was Charlene's father. He was a large man with a high, jutting chest and gray whiskers that stuck out from his face in thorny clusters. He was so large that Wade felt like a child when he stood next to him. His father-in-law turned and lurched forward into the dark, a hand straying toward the railing but never quite touching it. Wade stretched himself and the soreness that had laid dormant now ran like a thumping current through his body. He rose and walked in the direction of Charlene's swaying father.

During his slumber he had been dreaming of her. Her dark, unguarded eyes swam before him in various forms, her resigned admonishments echoed down blurred corridors. Commingled with her quietude and disappointment were six numbers that stood out to him as clear as a gash of coal earth on a snowy bank, six sleep numbers: 8, 42, 9, 21, 10, 88. They had come to him pure and infinite. He would have to call Charlene the next time the tug came to port. She would get word to Dee and ask her if she wouldn't mind buying a lottery ticket in New Orleans—for lottery sales were illegal in Mississippi—8, 42, 9, 21, 10, 88, those were the numbers. He must remember and she must remember too. It seemed crazy, by why couldn't the winning numbers come to him in this way? Who was to say? Were the young and forlorn of this earth not meant to dream dreams?

Chapter 22

A sudden breeze shook and then billowed the plastic banner that stood over the gathering on the side lawn of St. Andrew's church. The sign read, "St. Andrew's Annual Lenten Fish Fry." At the lower right-hand corner of the banner was the reminder, "Sponsored by your parish Knights of Columbus."

On one side of the yard was a row of cafeteria-style tables behind which stood a gathering of men in plastic body aprons and paper chef hats. On the other side of the tables there were fifty or so people, mostly women, talking and holding empty plates in their hands. Father Hemmler sat, with one leg crossed over his knee, looking sadly into the horizon as a plump woman chattered in his ear about the need for a nursery for at least one of the Masses.

"Considering we don't have a crying room, I think it's a service that the church needs to provide, not only for the parents and children but also for the other adults who attend Mass."

She paused, taking a sip from a diet soft drink which she held, wrapped in a paper napkin, in her hand.

"A Mass seems so much more . . . authentic if it's not interrupted by the cries of children. Not that I am opposed to children—not at all—but some parents just don't know how to control them. My kids would not so much as blink when they were in church—they knew the consequences. And, believe me, they'd have the same reverence for Mass to this day, if they were still Catholic. . . ."

Her voice rose above the steady murmuring of the others. Jackie stood over the three-bay deep fryer with a plastic bowl filled to the brim with breaded catfish.

"You ain't got dat thing hooked up yet?" he asked.

His voice fell down to Stewart, who was laying on the ground beneath the fryer trying to attach the hose of a butane tank to its underside. Percy knelt beside him, the deep green grass discoloring the knees of his pants.

"Tell him if he asks that question one more time, I may strike him," Stewart said.

Percy looked over the metal frame of the fryer.

"Stewart says if you ask that question one more time he may strike you," Percy said.

The other Knights laughed, appreciatively.

"Well, come on den. Dese fish are going to go rancid. They can't stay in the outdoors like dis all day," Jackie said.

Stewart called to Percy, who stooped back under the table, listened, and then looked up, blushing, and then stooped back down again to Stewart.

"I can't tell him that," he whispered down to Stewart. "The ladies are here."

Suddenly the hose of the nozzle, which had proven so vexing before, slipped easily onto the brass grooves of the stove. Stewart tightened the cuff with rising spirits.

"Fixed," he said and popped up from the ground. "Crank up the jets, boys."

Three hands reached for the two red knobs on the front of the fryer. The butane hissed up to the pilot light and then exploded in a soft combustion under the steel plate.

"It should only take a minute to reheat," Stewart said to Jackie. "And, hey, whatever ya'll eat, you pay for, okay?"

"Right, Stew," someone answered for the group.

Stewart walked to the edge of the tables and clapped his hands.

"Taking orders," he called.

A deep breath of relief was emitted from the crowd. They formed a line as quickly as politeness would allow— barely allow. But the first person in line, the woman who had been discussing the nursery, blushed and then grandly announced: "Shouldn't Father be the first to be served?"

She swept him to the front with a broad movement of one arm. It was a great sacrifice. She was very hungry.

Jackie looked at the line and began happily dropping the fish into the roiling oil.

"Ease them in gently," Benjamin Gauchet cautioned. It was his first year directing the preparation and cooking of the fish fry and already he felt that his ancient family's recipe and procedures were being violated in unspeakable ways.

Percy was collecting tickets from the crowd that was now growing quite large. He would take a ticket, smile broadly like a child with a prize, open the lid of a cigar box, place the ticket inside, and then close the box. Other men took the plates from the people and began heaping them full of coleslaw, creole string beans, and bread.

"Fishes and loaves, fishes and loaves, that's what we're all about here," one Knight sang out merrily.

"Condiments to the left," Stewart said, directing the patrons with the swirling hand of a traffic cop to a table filled with packets of ketchup, tartar sauce, and lemon juice.

Within a half hour, the line of diners was moving swiftly past the tables and more were arriving in the parking lot.

"Hello, sweetheart," Dee said, coming before him with a full plate. She pinched off a piece of the catfish and placed it in Stewart's mouth.

Stewart closed his eyes and swayed slightly.

"Good, huh?" Dee asked Stewart.

"Unprecedented," he declared. "Truly, I'm having a hard time finding a downside to Bobby Melancon's death. After his retirement there was not much left for him to live for anyway. He received last rites. His wife is obviously much happier now that he's gone, and our fish fry has improved exponentially."

"Oh, Stewart!" Dee said and then took another bite. "You might be right."

A line of diners had formed behind Dee, holding their Styrofoam plates and looking around her at the boxes of condiments in silent desperation.

"Condiment line detours around my wife," Stewart said.

"Oh," Dee said, taking another bite and stepping aside. "Sorry."

She stripped off another piece of fish and laid it in his mouth.

"Charlene called me this morning," she said.

Stewart let the strip hang from his mouth like a deflated balloon.

"Fear not. Wade is still on the boat," she said. "She just called to say 'Hello.'"

Stewart still let the dough hang.

"Not collect," she added. "Okay, collect, but under three minutes."

Stewart sucked in the strip of fish like a strand of spaghetti.

"She also gave me a set of numbers—8, 42, 9, 21, 10, 60 . . . something like that. . . . I wrote them down. She said Wade dreamed them while he was on the boat. They just stood out in the air before him, like some kind of vision or something—so I bought a lottery ticket for him. Wouldn't it be exciting if those were the winning numbers? It's up to seventy million now, you know. That is almost a record."

"Dee the chances are—"

"So slim they're almost they're almost invisible," Dee said. "I know, you always say that. Oh, Stewart, I know it's so foolish but just think for a few dollars a week they have that great hope in their lives."

"They could save that money and buy something that they really need," Stewart. "Like food, for instance."

"Or they could have hope," Dee said. "Hope is a kind of food for some people."

She broke off another piece of fish and put it in her own mouth.

"Oh, really? In that case, next year I am going to give up hope for Lent instead of red meat and sausage," Stewart said. (His only animal protein since Mardi Gras had been seafood. The sacrifice was killing him.)

"Wade swears that if he ever wins the lottery, he will give you half of it."

"Are these my asbestos Dockers?" Stewart asked. "I hope so, because it's like that seventy million . . . seventy million, right? It's like it's burning a hole in my pocket. At this point, I would settle for fifty dollars a week in installment payments for groceries and electricity already rendered."

Dee stuck another portion of fish into his mouth.

"I'm going to the condiment table," she said.

"Gambling is a vice, by the way," Stewart called after her. "Except for the youth ministry bingo and our upcoming bass boat raffle to benefit the seminarian fund. Those are good causes, and the Lord enjoys his people losing money for good causes. But have you ever seen a real gambler, like from a casino? They cringe and blink like a mole when you take them out into natural light. They have no idea what time or even what day it is."

Stewart curved his shoulders and bent nearly in double, bringing his wrist close against his chest and giving himself T-Rex arms. He quivered and made a sickening face.

A tall man, thin and serious suddenly appeared in front of him.

"Condiments?"

Stewart straightened and quickly pointed to the table.

Dee shook her head. It was good to be out. The house seemed almost hostile to her now. Tim and Amy's rooms stood as rigid entities, unwilling to adapt to the new reality. Any new furniture Dee attempted to bring was met with what felt like scorn from the walls, a crushing threat from the ceiling. When Dee moved her sewing machine into Amy's room, the mismatch felt so acute she could not complete a single stitch there. Stewart tried to paint the walls of Tim's room and only got so far as filling in the holes left from the posters of half-naked and snarling rock stars Tim had hung there. Any color, even the same hue, looked grossly out of place there.

These were still Tim and Amy's rooms—and always would be.

And the addition. Stewart wondered why he ever thought he needed all that room. Even if he did modify things so he could park the Ranger in it, there were still chunks of leftover space in an area that had once seemed so cramped and confining. Many times, Dee put her face close to the glass of the small window above her kitchen sink, expecting to see Charlene in the yard minding the children. Often Stewart would come bounding down the hall and then stop like a man whose mind had been just wiped clean of all thought, desire, or memory, but who still retained a vague feeling that something was missing. They both often started and then stopped.

Each week a letter would arrive from Amy, and she would seem farther and farther away, her words struggling in a sincere but increasingly futile effort to surmount the growing distance and detachment of time and space. It was as if a fissure had opened at her feet and was yawning into an ever-widening separation between her and her former life. Tim never communicated with them at all and, to Stewart anyway, it was starting to feel as if he had never existed underneath their roof. He found this feeling most disturbing and disorienting. Calls went back and forth between San Diego, California, and New Orleans, Louisiana. These calls were most anticipated and welcome but, Dee had learned, phone calls and letters alone could not bring children back home.

Chapter 23

Stewart looked up with a start from the bowl of cereal he was eating.

"These numbers just came to me—10, 29, 89. They just popped into my mind, unbidden."

Dee glanced up from the newspaper she was reading as it lay open, flat against the table.

"That's today's date," she said.

Stewart chewed thoughtfully.

"Okay, but it is still six digits if separated into single units. Those could be the winning numbers. A date is just as good as the serial number on a bag of rice, wouldn't you say?"

He was not taking his near encounter with untold wealth very well at all.

"I can buy a ticket today, if you want," Dee said.

Stewart made an unnatural sound.

"No, don't! They'll do it to me again. None of the numbers will match or they will be one digit off. Who knows what their dark arts will conjure. My arteries cannot take the strain. Several have hardened to brick already."

He returned morosely to the bowl of cereal in front of him, the pieces of which were disintegrating in the milk. Then he looked up again.

"Or those will be the winning numbers because I didn't buy a ticket," he moaned. He rubbed his stomach. "I think I caught Jackie's angina."

"Doesn't that affect your heart?" Dee said.

"Sometimes; it can be system-wide," Stewart said. "A real widow maker."

"Stewart, eat your oat bran and don't worry about it," Dee said, smiling secretly and turning the page of the newspaper. "I'll go down and buy a ticket today."

"No!" Stewart said. "That's exactly what they want you to do. That is how you get trapped and the next thing you know you are selling plasma to support your gambling habit."

"Stewart, the ticket costs a dollar. I think your plasma is worth more than that."

"The best thing we can do is pick the numbers we think have no chance of winning and then we buy . . . no . . . no . . . we don't buy a ticket, because that is part of their trap, you see. No, we pick the wrong numbers and buy a ticket—I mean we don't buy a ticket. That's our best chance. You have to be strategic about this."

The winning number for the drawing that evening was Stewart's license plate number. He buried his face into the shag rug in the center of their living room. It smelled warmly of food and feet. At this level the long-haired fibers of the rug appeared as stalks of grain before his watering eyes. It did not seem to be an unpleasant world in which to live.

"We are healed of a suffering only by experiencing it to the full," he said into the rug. "That's Proust, if any of you mites or detritus in your little shag world care."

The telephone in the kitchen rang and Dee rose to answer it.

"Well, is he alright?" Stewart heard Dee ask.

He took his face out of the rug and noted the troubled look on Dee's face, her tightened brows and pale cheeks. He rose and walked into the kitchen.

"Who?" Stewart asked.

Dee turned her back to him and put a finger to one ear.

"Uh-huh. Did they find the man who did it?" she asked.

"Did what?" Stewart asked.

She slapped his words away.

He stuck his quizzical visage directly in front of her face.

"Did what?" he asked.

"He doesn't remember at all? That's terrible. He could have been drowned."

"Who?" Stewart asked. "Who could have been drowned?"

Dee stuck a hand in front of his face.

"How long do they think he will have to stay in the hospital?"

"Who?!" Stewart demanded.

"Still, Charlene, I think you should notify the police," Dee said.

Stewart threw his hands above his head. That explained it. Wade had gotten drunk and landed into some sort of trouble. He walked to the sink and fished out a glass from the drain, intending to fix himself a Coke.

"Well, why wouldn't we want you to come back?" Dee asked.

Stewart dropped the glass into the sink. It shattered into pieces. He turned and faced Dee. His eyes bugged and his skin strained until it looked waxen. Dee had turned to face him when she heard the breaking glass, now she turned back around.

"No, of course. You know y'all are welcomed back here anytime," she said.

Stewart ran around to face her, shaking his head repeatedly and mouthing, "No. No. No. No. No."

"Yes. Yes," Dee said. "Definitely. I don't have to ask Stewart; I know what he would say. The addition is just sitting there. Uh-huh. Oh, sure he could find work here, no doubt."

Stewart pulled up the front of his hair, stuck out a dead man's tongue and began to spin around like a mad ballerina. Dee had to turn her back and face the refrigerator door to stop from laughing. He rushed to the sink and began filling a large pot full of water.

"Listen to that rain, Dee," he yelled. "Sure hope it doesn't flood again like yesterday. What a mess that was. Apocalyptic. Interstate floated away. Telephone poles strewn like pick-up sticks. It's a miracle our phone line still works."

"So, how's the newcomer adjusting to the tribe?" Dee asked.

Stewart brought the pot filled with water across the kitchen to Dee. He flicked some water on her to get her attention. She turned, frowned, and shook her head. Stewart looked at the phone and then back at the pot of water he now held before her.

"Terrible storm, Dee, worse than Betsy, worse than Camille," he called as if from far off. "Throw it in," he whispered urgently.

"He's doing fine. The weather? Oh, yes, it's raining cats and dogs here," Dee said.

Stewart's eyes brightened and he raised the pot of water closer to the phone. Dee worked her way around him stretching the long cord until she was in the hallway.

"Oh, my gosh, the O'Neils' above-ground pool just swept past us," he shouted over his shoulder. "With Mrs. O'Neil in it. She's lost weight."

He walked to the hallway and held the pot so close to the telephone the tip of the mouthpiece was nearly touching the water's surface.

"Yeah," Dee said. "I'll call you back to see how he's doing. Okay. Stewart sends his love. Yes, I will tell him. Okay. Yeah. Sure thing. Bye-bye, sweetheart."

Dee brought the receiver to her waist.

"Did you want to tell me something?"

Stewart raised the pot threateningly towards her. She squealed, hopped out of the way, ran back into the kitchen, and skipped across the floor to the sink, hanging the phone up along the way.

"Stewart, put down the pot and unclench your nostrils, please."

Stewart did as he was told. His shoulders slumped and he walked to the sink. He tipped the pot forward and let the water run out of its side. The shattered glass crinkled beneath the water.

"What happened?" he asked.

"Wade was out late one night—"

"Drinking?" Stewart said.

"Drinking," Dee affirmed.

"Special occasion? Big promotion? Award night?"

"This is serious, Stewart. He could have been killed. Some thug jumped him and beat him up really badly. He threw Wade into the Gulf. He had to swim ashore with five busted ribs and a fractured wrist. He's got a deep gash below his eye that needed ten stitches. Charlene says he'll be in the hospital at least another day. They have to do some kind of brain scan on him."

"Do they want to come here?" Stewart asked.

"You know the answer to that. I swear Stewart, they have the worse luck. Wade doesn't like working on the boat. He's scared out there. He says Charlene's dad is cruel to him and Charlene agrees. And now this happens and the baby, Jude Hope, needs some operation the doctor says."

"What operation?" Stewart said.

"Oh, it's something with her chin. It's for cosmetic purposes and Charlene's dad says he won't give them a dime for it unless it's a medical emergency. But you don't want the baby going through life with an ugly chin—not a little girl. They just have it so hard."

"We can help with the operation," Stewart said.

Dee looked at him.

"How, Stewart? I mean, I'd love to, but we can't afford much."

"I mean we, the Knights. We raised over one thousand dollars with our fish fry and another five thousand dollars with the raffle. They can have that. I don't suppose we'll ever get to wear those uniforms."

Chapter 24

The day Wade and Charlene moved back to New Orleans it rained violently. For hours gusts of warm wind swept a wall of falling water horizontally against the Georges' home. Rain clattered on the slate roof and drained down the clapboard siding in thick rivulets. The O'Neils' above-ground pool did not become airborne, but it did buckle with the excess of water and force of wind, concaving and spilling its contents, which did not include Mrs. O'Neil, into the Georges' backyard. Dark, fetid water rose knee-deep on the streets of their neighborhood. Wade and Charlene waited out the storm in the driveway, which was slightly higher than the streets. They had arrived in a fading green Buick they had bought for seven hundred dollars from a friend of Charlene's father. They waved from inside the dark car and Wade held the baby up to the dripping glass for inspection. Stewart and Dee waved back from their porch but could hardly see anything through the sheets of silver rain. Dark, shadowy forms, which each took to be those of the other children, jostled in the backseat. At one point, the distinct white soles of a child's sneakers stomped violently against the driver's rear side window.

After more time passed, the front passenger's window cracked open slightly and a thin line of smoke escaped from inside the vehicle. Darren opened the back door and made a hesitant attempt to exit the vehicle before being hollered at and driven back inside the car by the pelting rain and an explosive peal of thunder and forked lightning. More shoving ensued in the backseat. Dwight cried as steadily and as unceasingly as Darren and David fought one another. Hope slept on the frayed seat between her parents. Stewart and Dee retreated to the house when the wind changed direction and the rain beat down directly onto the porch. They ate their lunch standing in the front doorway and looking out at the car through a glassed, screen door.

The rain persisted into the afternoon, popping off the roof of the car, gurgling down its bumpers. The water from the street rose halfway up their wheels. Leaves and grass clippings swirled in the eddies of the street. The newly planted "ham and eggs" inside the front yard's landscaping tires floated and circled the tree trunks like little arcade ducklings. Blackbirds came fluttering down to roost on the telephone wire that stretched in front of the

Georges' home. Hunched against the unrelenting rain, they appeared as dark-coated sentries on a forbidding watch.

From Charlene's account on the phone that morning, things had been going better for them. The money Wade received as an employee of the tugboat paid for most of his medical expenses. Hope had been able to have her operation thanks to the Knights' help and, except for a light rouge around her chin and two already fading lines from the incision curving down from the corner of her mouth, appeared perfectly normal. Most encouragingly, Wade had been attending a church-sponsored substance abuse program which he had signed up for with no prompting or prodding from anyone. He had been attending its twice-weekly meetings faithfully and had not had a drink for a month.

Stewart approached the car once in boots and a large umbrella, but the wind swooped under it, turned its canvas dome upward and shattered its steel ribs. The entire family within the car burst into laughter at the sight. Stewart could hear their muffled glee as he headed back to the porch. Minutes later, the back door of the Buick buckled and David and Darren emerged, sloshed through the waist-high water with delight and made their way to the house. Next came Charlene racing with Dwight in her arms, followed by Wade, trekking slowly toward the house with Hope close to his chest and covered with one of Charlene's blankets.

Stewart held the sagging remnant of his umbrella over

the group as they came up the front steps. Dee dispatched towels to the dripping crowd, who settled in the living room. Charlene and Dee buffed the children dry as Wade and Stewart dried themselves. Afterwards, Wade, with the towel affixed atop his head like a turban, watched as Stewart repaired the umbrella with tiny pliers and some soldering wire.

"Ya'll catch any more parades after we left?" Wade asked.

Stewart shook his head.

"I caught the nutria, though. The wildlife removal team came and got him. The Nuisance Wildlife Control operator congratulated me on the design of the trap. They took photos."

"They said they'd like to copy Stewart's design and pay him for it," Dee said.

"Whoa, bro!" Wade said. His right hand was encased in ace bandaging that encircled a blue plastic splint.

"Stewart wouldn't sell it to them," Dee said.

"Not for the pittance they were asking. Besides, since I pay city and state taxes, selling my invention to a municipal body would be tantamount to me buying my own invention with my own money which is perverse even to the most Keynesian-addled mind."

Charlene laughed.

"Thank you, Charlene," Dee said.

"Those words of his," Charlene said, shaking her head in a cloud of smoke.

"It's true," Stewart protested, but only mildly. He had now figured out just how to fix the umbrella and knew that, with a little time, he could have it working as good as new. He was disproportionately happy with this outcome, but he did not want to discuss the trap anymore. He grew suddenly morose.

"Let me see that baby again," Dee said. She took Hope from the blanket she was lying on in the middle of the floor and brought the child to her arms. "Aw, she's beautiful. Beautiful. Beautiful!" Dee proclaimed.

"So, Stewart, I hear you got a date for me to take that civil service test for the post office," Wade said eagerly.

Stewart strung together a few more of the umbrella's ribs in silence.

"They're giving the test April ninth. That's a Saturday. Two weeks," Stewart said. "I can give you some books to study that will help you. It's a pretty tough test."

"It's for government work; how tough can it be?" Wade laughed and so did Dee and Charlene and the children. Even Hope caught the merriment and gurgled a laugh. Only Stewart remained silent. He looked intently at his work and pulled the wire he was placing between the umbrella's netting fast. He pulled more wire from a coil and snapped it angrily between the metal pinchers of the pliers. He had reason for being angry. Just moments before he had smelled the sweet/sour and unmistakable odor of alcohol on Wade's eager breath.

Chapter 25

The man was bald, well-kept, and meticulous in every detail. His chestnut-colored skin was scrubbed and burnished to a high sheen that captured the fluorescent overhead office light and reflected it back in soft yellow ovals that appeared at his forehead and cheekbones. He wore a starched, white linen shirt with a Nehru collar.

"You, please be quiet," he said, calling over the classroom. "Take seats, please. You, please be quiet. You, please come to order."

For a moment after his announcement, the noise level inside the classroom, which was located within the city's community college, increased exponentially as people hurriedly finished their conversations. Desks moved and nearly tipped over as some oversized patrons took their seats.

"Please come to order," the man said again. "Test is

about to begin."

The stirring and disorder ceased, and the classroom was perfectly quiet.

"This is the civil service test for employees of the United States Postal Service," the man said. "Total test time will be exactly three hours."

As he spoke, two men began handing a thick booklet to each seated applicant. When one of the men came to Wade's desk, he found that its occupant had his head resting on his arms, which lay folded against the surface of the desk. The man paused for a moment and then slipped the booklet underneath the sleeper's arms and proceeded to the next desk. Wade roused reluctantly at the intrusion of the booklet.

"The test consists of three parts, each with a time limit of fifty minutes. The last section of the test is . . ."

Wade shifted groggily in his seat and began thumbing through the pages of the booklet. He took out the answer sheet which contained hundreds of tiny ovals with the letter A, B, C, D, or E printed within them. Wade took his pencil and began randomly shading ovals.

"Please! Test had not started! Test had not started, sir!!" the man called excitedly.

All eyes turned toward Wade, who continued his idle shading.

"Please. Take his answer sheet," the man directed one of his helpers.

By this time Wade realized he was the cause of the

commotion. He handed his answer sheet to the helper with a wide, curving grin.

The man sliced the sheet into long strips directly in front of Wade, then crumped the collection and deposited it into a wastepaper basket at the front of the classroom. He then brought Wade a new test sheet. The woman who was seated in front of Wade glared at him for an extended moment before she spun around in her seat to attend to the continuing instructions.

"It is recommended to answer as many of the questions as possible. If you don't know the answer to a question move on to the next one. You can always come back and answer the question later. Remember the test is based on the percentage of those question answered correctly and any blank space is an incorrect answer. Now please turn to the first section of test. You have two minutes to read the instructions and then the timer is set."

Wade looked at the two thick paragraphs of directions.

"You got to be kidding," he mumbled.

"Shhh!" said the woman in front of him.

As Wade skimmed the set of directions, his glance fell to a small box at the corner of the answer sheet. It contained a row of ovals. The first oval had been checked. The next oval had only a small section of its center shaded. Another oval had been darkly shaded beyond its borders. Still a fourth oval had a large X planted within its borders. The final oval was a perfectly shaded egg. Underneath this oval was the word "Correct" and the caveat, "Use a No. 2 lead pencil only."

The other ovals were labeled, "Incorrect."

The instructor held a white timer with a large knob on its face above his head.

He turned the knob one revolution and a tiny ring emitted from it.

"Begin!" he shouted.

Wade shaded the first oval on the answer sheet a light, translucent gray so that you could clearly see the "A" beneath the thin film of graphite. For question number two, Wade selected oval "E" and proceeded to draw a smiling face on it. He shaded all five ovals a heavy dark black for question number three. He left question five's ovals blank. The ovals for question six were painted the color of dyed Easter eggs thanks to Wade's use of his four-color pen.

After each section of the test was completed, the group was told they could go to the restroom or stretch beside their desk or take a walk down the hall for a few minutes. Wade fell promptly back to sleep with his ace bandaged arm covering his face. When the timer sounded to mark the end of the last section of the test, Wade was hunched over his answer sheet filling in ovals at a feverish pace.

"Time. Please. Time," the instructor said.

Wade lifted up the test paper and cocked his head slightly with satisfaction. A panoramic view of the sheet showed a fat birthday cake composed entirely of shaded ovals. A single, burning candle rose from the cake's crest. One of the helpers took the sheet from his hand and placed it, without comment, in the stack of other papers he had gathered. On the trip home from the test, Wade's arm began to throb and his headache from the prior night's drinking had not gone away. He pulled the Buick into a convenience store parking lot and purchased two glass quarts of beer. He had switched to beer lately, believing it to be some kind of step-down drug toward complete sobriety.

Charlene was knitting a blanket when he came home. The quilt walls had been rehung and their sparse belongings had been placed in order. She sat in the dark tent of their bedroom working steadily. A hazy glow emitted from the television in the corner. Wade sat in the wicker rocker across the room from her. He cast one leg over the arm of the chair and broke the seal of one of the quarts.

"How'd the test go?" Charlene asked.

"Piece of cake," Wade said. He turned the quart upside down and pressed it against his lips.

"Who's the blanket for?" he asked after he completed the first long pull from the bottle.

"Mrs. Townsend's grandbaby," Charlene said. "He was born with only one lung."

She fluffed out the ends of the blanket so that her work lay flat against her knees and legs.

"Pretty," Wade said. "Can you live with one lung?"

"I think so," Charlene said. "But you got to have at least one."

Wade took another long drink from the bottle. The light from the television provided just enough illumination to show his reflection in the swarthy surface of the bottle's glass. The face it showed was surrealistic. Only his forehead, the tip of his nose and his chin were visible. His eyes were two dark orbs, and his cheeks and other features were lost in the curve of the bottle.

"Charlene, you remember that time we rode in the alley at Catahoula Creek?" Wade asked.

"The first day we met," Charlene said.

"That weren't the first time," Wade said, harshly. "I met you before that at the skating rink."

"I don't remember," Charlene said.

"Well, I did. You was with that Molly girl. The one with all that crazy red hair."

"Molly Hanikel?" Charlene asked.

"Whatever," Wade said. "I met y'all over by the concessions stands. Me and you even skated a song together."

"I have no recollection of that," Charlene said.

"Anyway, you remember the ride in the alley?"

Charlene's eyes flashed up and then back down to the blanket.

"How could I forget? Them people nearly killed us."

"Yeah, that's what I been thinking about," Wade said. "Two minutes before, those people were our friends. I had been drinking with most of them that afternoon. They all knew who we were, and we knew who they were."

Wade turned the bottle on his knee so that the wet label of the beer showed rather than his reflection.

"I remember in school once they told us that the parts

of the brain that control love and hate are just inches apart—not even inches, really, centipedes or centimeters, whatever, apart. The space between them is smaller than the tip of my fingernail. That's how it was with them people along the alley—one minute they was our friends and the next minute they was trying to knock us out with sticks."

"They were cruel," Charlene said.

"Their control had shifted," Wade said. "An inch or a fraction of an inch."

He took another drink from the bottle, plunging the foamy head well below the halfway mark.

"So, I'm thinking, if less than an inch separates things that seem far away from one another like love and hate, then there may be only a little that separates other things like success and failure, or winning or losing, or sadness and happiness. In the classes at that church, they told me alcoholics have to hit rock bottom before they can see their way to crawl out. Now, I've been falling all this time so maybe I am just an inch, maybe just a fraction of an inch from bouncing off the bottom. And if I am that close to the bottom, can I really be that far from the top?"

"What if you break through the bottom?" Charlene said. "How far you reckon you can fall?"

"It's not a bottom like glass," Wade said. "It's a rock bottom. You can't break through rock."

"How do you know you can bounce off it, then?" Charlene said.

Wade took a final drink from the bottle. He drank so

deeply that bubbles filled his nose and his eyes watered.

"You can bounce," Wade said. "If you can fall, then you can bounce. I have to think like that. Charlene, with that lottery our lives could change just so instantly and completely."

His eyes shone wistfully.

"But you reckon we'll have anything left after we done all that changing?" he asked. "I mean, you and me?"

Charlene stopped knitting.

"That man that beat you up," Charlene said. "He used to like me in school. I bet he still does. I bet that's the way he thinks you get a girl, by hurting somebody—like them big mooses on them wildlife shows. That's the way most men think. They think you got to be mean. Men are mean."

Wade was looking directly at her.

"You aren't mean, Wade. You done a lot of nothing, but you ain't never done nothing mean. Stewart ain't mean either. I guess that runs in the family."

Wade nodded.

"I think Stewart and me are basically the same type of people. We just think differently about things. Take different approaches."

"Stewart ain't no drunk," Charlene countered. "He's a churchman."

"Stewart drinks organization," Wade said. "He drinks order and power. He drinks all them kinds of things that I would not put my lips to. And church? Who knows? Maybe I got more faith than Stewart. He's always running about ordering them Knights of his around, arguing with the parish council, spearheadin' this and that as if God needed him to keep the show going, keep the world spinning on its axle."

Wade turned up the bottle again and let the residual suds slide down its neck into his mouth.

"Look how he is with Mass. Always arriving a half hour before it starts. What does he need to do? Nudge God awake before the company arrives? Me, I don't need to take a Mass to prove there's a God. I just got to open my eyes."

Wade slipped his hand down the arm of the chair and let the empty bottle down slowly onto the concrete flooring. His hand wandered over the space above the floor and found the stem of the other bottle.

"And one day, I'll open my eyes and see those winning numbers, and then everyone will see," he said.

"What makes you so sure you'll pick the right numbers?" Charlene said. "How come you're so certain?"

"I just know it," Wade said. "Besides, I was lucky enough to pick you, weren't I?"

Charlene worked her needles steadily.

I ain't no winner, she thought. I'm a stupid girl. I used to be kind of good looking but not so much anymore. But I will always be with Wade, I guess, whether he bounces off that rock bottom, cracks his head wide open on it, or finds some way to crash through it and keep falling forever.

Chapter 26

Dee pushed the shopping cart along the row bordered by cereal boxes on one side and cake mixes, sugar, and coffee on the other. Charlene was behind her pushing a cart filled with children. Hope lay squeezed snugly in a carrier within the only part of the cart that was actually made to carry children. The twins stood in the cart like sailors against a bulwark, their hands outstretched grasping at the multi-colored enticements they passed. Dwight sat on the bottom rack of the cart, silent and dull-eyed.

"No. No. No," Charlene said mechanically, as the boys reached with renewed optimism at every product that caught their eyes.

"Darren, no!" Charlene suddenly shouted.

Dee heard the soft tapping of boxes hitting the waxed floor. She turned and saw that Darren was leaning nearly completely out of the cart. David held the soles of his shoes against the rim of the cart, supporting his climb to crime. Darren had a box of Cap'n Crunch in one hand, with the other he gripped the edge of the shelf.

"David, let him go," Charlene ordered.

For what might have been the first time in his young life, David immediately obeyed one of his mother's directives and released his hold on his brother's feet. Darren went crashing like a wrecking ball into the shelf. Products scattered, slid, and popped against the floor. Darren clung to the top shelf wailing. David gave a surprised look and then retreated to the back of the cart, cowering in the space beneath the suspended Hope. Charlene broke Darren's grip and, holding him by the arms, swung him back into the cart. He wailed even more loudly and inconsolably. Dee began picking up the fallen boxes, plastic bottles, and packages.

"You know, Charlene, I could really do the shopping for both families by myself. It'd probably be easier for you and the children," Dee said.

"Oh, I am glad to help out," Charlene said.

Dee looked at her as she picked up a row of cereal boxes.

"Well, it could have been eggs, right?" Dee said.

"Or syrup."

"True."

They turned at the end of the aisle and started down another. Dee checked her list and began pulling goods from both sides of the shelves.

"Chili with beans or without?" she called over her shoulder.

"Beans give Wade gas," Charlene said.

Dee placed the can back on the shelf and reached for another.

"Definitely without," she said.

"How about soup?"

"Chicken noodle's fine. Any kind," Charlene said, "Darren, I'm warning you stay in this cart. One, two, three . . ."

Dee strolled ahead, mouthing the numbers in anticipation.

"Five," she said and cringed as a row of cans crashed to the floor. Darren was suddenly at her side presenting her with a can of chili, with beans. Dee took the can from him.

"Okay, but keep them away from Daddy. And Uncle Stewart, too, come to think of it."

A woman in a grapefruit themed muumuu and a silk scarf covering a head full of hair rollers came into their aisle.

"What a beautiful child," she declared. "Is he yours?"

"Almost," Dee said.

The woman smiled in friendly incomprehension and moved on, nodding to Charlene as she passed her. When they emerged from the supermarket, Dee's cart was filled with bagged groceries that fluttered in the wind as a breeze raced across the parking lot. Charlene followed with her cart. Each of the children held a dripping red popsicle in their hands, lapping them as quickly as possible as the treats rapidly diminished in the hot sun.

Charlene held two unwrapped popsicles clenched by the sticks between her teeth—one for her and one for Dee. Dee put the groceries in the bed of the truck while Charlene secured the children in the cab in a variety of baby seats, boosters, and seatbelts. After the children were safely stowed, she turned to help Dee with the groceries. They both grabbed one bag at the same time.

"I got this one," Dee said hurriedly, but Charlene had already commandeered it.

"What is it, a surprise?" Charlene asked. She gazed into the bag. "Dee George!"

Dee crimsoned.

"I'm not even late. I just have a hunch is all."

"Oh, I've seen this sucker before," Charlene said, taking the home pregnancy test from the bag and reading a line of the directions. "A positive result from this test is only one indication that you are pregnant. For definitive results consult your physician, unless your name is Charlene Perkins Terry, in which case get ready to balloon."

"Please put it down," Dee said. She didn't know who she feared might see or hear them.

Charlene put the box back into the bag.

"And right next to the pickles."

"Don't tease me," Dee said. "You have no idea . . ."

Charlene took a step back when she saw Dee's face redden and her eyes suddenly turning bloodshot.

"I'm not—Dee," she said. "I'm sorry."

She presented one of the popsicles to her.

"Here, I got a treat for you even," she said.

Dee accepted the treat wearily. She worked the red ice into her mouth and looked over the bed of the truck at the crowded parking lot.

"It ain't the same is it?" Charlene asked.

"What?" Dee said.

"Having foster kids ain't the same as having your own baby, is it?"

Dee walked to the driver's side of the truck.

"I hope I can answer that question one day," she said.

Chapter 27

It was very hot. The heat seemed to be part and parcel of every piece of matter around Stewart. The street was a long riverbed of flat heat. Heat sang along the power lines above him. It crouched upon a glaring fire hydrant. It rose in glassy spirals from distant rooftops. It baked the letters inside his mailbag. It was Saturday and, despite the weather, people were outside. Teenage girls laid out on plastic lawn loungers, offering their pale forms to the unremitting sun. Ladies in floppy hats and moistened work shirts spaded flower beds. Men grimaced behind blaring lawn mowers. Stewart plodded down the street and up the steps, feeding the empty mouths of countless mailboxes.

"Hope you don't have any bills," a man said, looking up from edging his lawn. "You can keep those."

The man laughed appreciatively at his own joke.

Stewart smiled weakly. A trace of sweat rolled from his forehead, down the slope of his face and into the crease of his neck. Several drops of perspiration fell from his hair and splashed on the bundle of letters he held in his left hand. Stewart thrust the bundle into the mailbox.

At the next house, a woman in a housecoat stood on the porch.

"Is my Roger Whittaker in there?" she snapped.

"Roger Whittaker?" Stewart asked.

"That's right," the woman said. "And before you say anything you should know that he sold more albums than the Beatles."

"I'm not surprised," Stewart said, "He could probably read music."

"Well, is he in there or not?" the woman asked.

Stewart reached into his bag and brought out two business size envelopes.

"Could he fit into these?"

The woman frowned and snatched the letters from him. Stewart shrugged and shifted the strap of his bag. He felt the wet strap fall against a dry portion of his shirt.

"No bills, I hope," said the man at the next house. He did not smile but looked sternly at Stewart. When Stewart handed him his mail, the man broke out in loud laughter.

"I'm picking at you, son. I'm picking at you," he said.

Stewart nodded, looked at the sun, and continued walking.

At the next house a maroon Mercedes Benz was cocked

in the driveway, its back half still in the street. The engine hummed quietly and the driver, a fortyish woman with black hair, brushed off her forehead and a beautiful, cold face, sat behind the wheel talking to her neighbor through the passenger window. As Stewart walked toward her home, she thrust an alabaster hand out of the unrolled driver's side window and continued the conversation with her neighbor, her faced turned away from Stewart. A jet stream of cool air gushed from the car's air-conditioned interior and fell against Stewart's chest. He lowered the stack of letters and a coiled *Vogue* magazine towards the woman's open hand. As the hand moved toward the packet, he pulled the stack away and set it against the right side of the car door's jamb. The hand moved to the right and Stewart pulled the letters away just as the hand grasped for the stack. The woman continued her animated conversation. He then tapped the mail stack gently against the opposite door jamb closest to the hood, attracting the hand back to that area, but when the hand reached for the letters, it closed upon empty air. Finally, the woman stopped talking and turned a hardened face toward him. Stewart moved the stack away from her hand and examined the top envelope closely.

"Is this 2306? Oh, my goodness. Wrong house. My bad."

He put the stack back in his bag and, renewed in spirit, nearly sprinted up to the next set of steps.

"Don't put any bills in there," a man called from the

roof of the house. He was pushing a rake handle down the length of a rain gutter that ran along the length of the roofline above Stewart. He grinned at Stewart through the tines of the rake.

"Don't fall off that roof," Stewart mumbled as he stuffed his mail into the black mailbox mounted next to the front door.

"If those are bills, nobody's home," said a young man standing in a large boat that rested on a trailer in the next-door driveway.

Sir Henri's house was next. Their housekeeper was sweeping the driveway with broad strokes that sent out white, swirling clouds of dust and grass clippings from the end of her broom. Sir Henri sat on his haunches at the end of the driveway. His pink tongue hanging slackly, he seemed oblivious to the encroaching dust cloud.

Stewart passed the sidewalk in front of the house. He lifted a pant leg exposing a pale, hairy limb.

"Here you go, Henri. *Limb du jour*. Come on, boy. Have a dig in. Come on. What's a few ruptured capillaries between old friends?"

The housekeeper stopped her sweeping. She held the broom in her big round hands.

"He don't want no part of you," the woman said. "You too crazy."

Her words were tinged with admiration.

"My mailman don't dress like that. He don't go shaking his leg in a dog's face or go tramping around people's backyards with a machine gun. You crazy," she laughed.

Stewart waved to her and scampered up the steps of the house, depositing in its mailbox the letters and magazine meant for the lady in the Mercedes Benz.

"Tell Sir Henri's owners that I read all of their postcards. Tell them sometimes I throw their paychecks in the canal. Tell them they once won a $100,000 drawing but the envelope just slipped through my hands and dissolved in a puddle."

The woman walked out from the covered portion of the drive and put a hand to her mouth.

"You crazy," she called. "Crazy."

Two houses down, an elderly woman hailed him as she snipped her hedge with a pair of hand clippers.

"If those are bills, you can keep them," she said, mirthfully waving the clippers.

Stewart gripped a section of his ribs.

"Mrs. Dubois, how do you keep coming up with those originals?" he said, chuckling extravagantly.

Mrs. Dubois waved at him with her clippers.

"Go 'head now," she said. "Did you bring me any free samples today? I'm nearly out of shampoo."

Stewart finished up his false laughter in a long whine and brought one slim pamphlet out of his bag. Mrs. Dubois opened the pamphlet and saw close-up, color photographs of pizzas with various toppings. One corner of the pamphlet showed a schematic of a pizza crust, a doughy dissection that displayed the distinct, multiple layers of the pie's foundation.

"Pizza!" she said. "I don't even like pizza. You can throw that in the trash can."

She folded the pamphlet and stuffed it back into Stewart's mailbag.

Stewart slogged through the rest of the route. Every inch of his shirt was now darkened a deeper hue by perspiration. Along the way he reached deep into his pants pocket and seized onto a worn, cedar rosary. He isolated one bead on the strand and squeezed it with all his might between his index finger and thumb, concentrating every thought, frustration, and dream in one pincer of prayer.

"Merciful, Lord," he prayed.

Chapter 28

Wade slipped one finger under the flap of the large yellow envelope and ran it down the length of paper, creating a jagged opening. He pulled a gray booklet from the package. Inside the booklet was a copy of his answer sheet and another smaller piece of paper that held his score and ranking. The copy of his answer sheet held the pattern of his cake, but the photocopy had been unable to bring out the diverse colors of Wade's four-color pen. Wade took the paper with his score and ranking and read:

> Dear Applicant:
> Your score out of a possible 100 points was 15.

Wade pursed his lips. Honestly, it was higher than he had anticipated. He continued to read:

Your national ranking for the Civil Service Test for Postal Employees is 1,540 out of 1,540. If you wish to retake this test you should contact the nearest post office or civil service entity in your area.

Wade returned the papers to the envelope without emotion. His arm had healed to the point that only a small ace bandage covering the upper part of his wrist was necessary.

"Come on, Dwight," Wade said, picking up the child, who was clad only in a diaper and a chili-stained t-shirt. He walked to the Buick and placed Dwight in the front seat next to him. He took a slip of paper, about the size of a receipt, from his breast pocket. It contained a list of numbers he had decided on the week before. He read the sheet over and dug his fingers into the crease formed where the car seat's back and base met. After some searching, he brought forth the stub of a pencil, whose eraser was nearly as long as its shaft. He laid the piece of paper on the dashboard and wrote the number 1540 on it. This took considerable effort given the limited space provided by both the dashboard and the smallness of the paper. Wade paused for a moment, looked reflectively into the distance and then back at Dwight.

"How old are you, son?" he asked.

Dwight looked at him, expressionlessly.

"Come on, show daddy how old you are," he pleaded.

The boy raised two fingers before him and then stuck them into his mouth.

"Yeah, that makes sense," he said and added the numeral "2" to the series of numbers, along with the boy's corresponding birth year.

"Okay, we'll give it a try," he said and began backing out the driveway.

Wade had both windows of the car rolled down. The wind created by the moving vehicle swirled about the backseat of the car, sucking school papers, candy wrappers, an empty potato chip bag and bits of broken crayon into a miniature tornado hovering above the vinyl. The wind buffeted the faces of both father and son and charged the moment with an inexplicable sense of joy. Dwight stood up on the seat and stomped his feet on the spongy, frayed surface, laughing at buoyancy. Wade alternately looked at the road and then at Dwight, occasionally poking his round belly, which stuck out from under his shirt.

The oyster shell drive popped and cracked loudly as Wade pulled the Buick beside the green brick exterior of the Trader's Lounge. The heretofore moribund bartender came alive as soon as he saw Wade enter carrying the boy under his arm like a surfer would hold his board.

"Uh, uh. No way. No minors," he said.

"He's alright," answered a woman sitting at the far end of the bar and holding a cigarette high in the air. She put the cigarette in her mouth and spoke around it.

"Here, hon, give him to me. Wade, that ain't no stack of books you carrying," she said.

She took Dwight from him and set him on the shelf of her expanded hips,

"Are you a good, boy?" she asked Dwight. "Tell the truth now, are you a good boy? Oh, I could just eat him up."

Dwight reached and moaned towards Wade but was soon

distracted by a bag of corn chips the woman rattled in front of him.

"I could lose my license," the man behind the bar said. "The ABC people don't go for kids in bars."

"You don't have a license, Alvin. They give those to bar owners, like my brother, not bartenders. You got one and half new customers. Try to treat them a little more hospitably. Especially a regular."

"A regular pain," the bartender mumbled.

Marie was the owner's sister, who acted like she owned the place. But if the real owner was here, he'd be a sight less welcoming to Wade. He'd bring up his longstanding, unpaid bar tab and half a dozen other objections to his presence, not to mention the kid. Wade walked to the section of the bar in front of Alvin and settled heavily on the stool. In front of him was a huge glass jar stacked with hard boiled eggs resting in brown vinegar. Strains of unidentified organic sediment floated in the liquid.

"Anybody ever buy one of those?"

The bartender glanced at the jar.

"Sometimes. What do you want?"

Wade shivered.

"All that vinegar. Ewww."

The bartender made no reply. Wade took the slip of paper out of his pocket and set it on the bar in front of him.

"Vodka, soda, and lime. In that order," Wade said, congenially.

The bartender grunted and made the drink. He set it

before Wade and put his hand beside it, thrusting two fingers forward. Wade slipped a five-dollar bill into the space between the two fingers. The ancient register, invisible in the gloom of the bar, clanged loudly as the bartender rang up the total. He placed the change next to Wade's drink. A penny rolled around in a circle on the thick varnish of bar's top and then dropped against it noiselessly.

"Got a pen?" Wade asked.

The bartender lifted his hand to his right ear instinctively and then turned toward the cash register. He brought back a pen with the name and address of a chiropractor printed on it. Wade took the pen, clicked it, and pointed to each number on the page. Almost immediately he drew a line through two of them. He took a sip from his drink and looked at the television screen. The Cubs were playing the Brewers. Wade looked at the bartender.

"Two to nothing, Cubs. Bottom of the second," the bartender said with effort.

Wade drew on his straw steadily until the glass was empty. He looked to his right. Dwight was seated on top of the bar, eating corn chips off its surface, and laughing at the antics of this strange, kind lady. Dwight would pick up a corn chip from the bar and then hold it in the air before his new friend. She would approach the chip wide-eyed and stiff-necked like a chicken and peck it from his hand. Each time she did this, Dwight pulled the empty hand back and stuck it in his mouth, laughing wildly.

"He likes you Marie," Wade said. He tapped the glass

with his index finger.

"One more, Alvin," he said.

Alvin made the drink, placed it next to Wade and took the payment out of the change he had placed on the bar just minutes before. Wade studied the three remaining series of numbers intently. One he had copied from an empty cigarette carton that had protruded from the heap at the top of their kitchen garbage can for days. The second series of numbers was the first few digits of the Buick's VIN number. The last numbers consisted of his aforementioned national ranking from the postal exam and the birth date of his second to youngest child. Wade focused on the numbers, waiting for them to speak. He picked his drink up and again began to steadily draw from it. Dwight's laughter continued to echo in the nearly empty room. Finally, Wade scratched out the cigarette carton and part of the VIN number.

"Okay, Alvin," he said.

"Another one?" Andy asked.

"No, a ticket. A lottery form. Y'all sell them, right?"

Andy opened the register with another loud clang, lifted the change tray, and pulled out a sheet from the bottom of the drawer. The sheet was filled with empty ovals, with a corresponding number beneath it. The bartender handed Wade the sheet.

"I need a pencil," Wade said. "It has to be a No. 2 lead."

"I need a dollar," the bartender said.

Wade glanced at the bar. Only a few coins remained

from his five-dollar bill. He reached into his pants pocket and brought forth a weathered bill.

"This one okay?" he asked.

Alvin came back with a short pencil with no eraser.

"Don't make any mistakes," he warned.

Wade glanced up from the page and gave him a wry grin. Then he began to shade each oval that contained his chosen numbers carefully.

"Just one ticket?" Alvin asked, watching his shading.

"It only takes one to win," Wade said.

He handed the completed sheet and pencil back to Alvin who looked at the selected numbers.

"Good luck," he said doubtfully.

Wade finished the drink with a gulp.

"Thanks," he said and walked to the end of the bar. "Come on, Dwighty."

Dwight protested the ending of the game with a moan.

"Thank Miss Marie for the snack and for watching you," Wade said. He had seated the boy on one shoulder.

"Say bye-bye," Wade said.

"Bye-bye," Dwight said.

"Goodbye, my love," Marie said, smoothing the front of his shirt. "Watch his little head on them fans," she warned. "Treat that child good. Teach him right from wrong and about God and his home in heaven and all that."

Wade nodded and walked out the door into the blazing sunlight which, refracted by the white pearl of the oyster shell parking lot, entered his eyes with a blinding vengeance.

Chapter 29

Dee knelt before a low table at the back of the small closet. A row of heavy winter clothing hung like a sanctuary curtain between her and the outside world. The only source of light was a naked bulb in the center of the closet ceiling. Before her was a short table covered with a soft white towel on which she had placed three small vials and the other appurtenances of the home pregnancy testing kit. The air in the closet was close but not unpleasant. She read the instructions once more. She was certain she understood them and could follow them precisely. The kit suggested that the best time to conduct the test was in the morning. That was still a half day and whole night away. This was the only direction she felt she would have trouble following. She sighed and then sighed again. She looked at the table once more. It was time to go. All this sneaking about was really silly. But if Stewart had seen the kit, she would have felt even sillier.

"Why?" he would have asked her with a consternated frown. Why would she torture herself so, after what the doctor had said and the infinitesimal odds he had offered. Why did she keep this up? He did not understand much about hope. He was not hostile to hope, he just found it such an unreliable ally in nearly all circumstances.

Dee stood up and parted the row of heavy clothes. She stepped through the space she had opened and felt for the light string, found it, and pulled down. The sudden, complete darkness was welcomed. She stepped over shoes and boxes toward the door, opened it and came face-to-face with Stewart.

"Wahhhh!" Dee yelled and jumped back.

Stewart blinked.

"Are you okay?"

"Like to give me a heart attack," Dee said. "I thought you were at Jackie's."

"I was," Stewart said. "And now I have inexplicably returned to my home. . . . What's wrong?"

Dee made an effort to compose herself. She was now vividly self-conscious, well aware of her own blushing and the secret at the back of the closet that now seemed to be jumping out of the door.

"Nothing," she said. "You just scared me, that's all." She moved away from the door.

"How is Jackie?"

"Querulous as ever," Stewart said, still eyeing her warily.

"Well, welcome home," Dee said. "Those are the ties for the rose bushes," she said, pointing to the nylon strips

Stewart held in his hand.

Stewart looked at his hand.

"Dee, we can't use these for the rose bushes," he said.

"Why not?"

Stewart held the strips before her as if the mere sight of them would make "Why not," manifestly clear.

"They're . . ."

"Old stockings," Dee said. "I was going to throw them into the trash."

"Which is exactly where they belong," Stewart said. "They are underwear. Don't you think it's a little titillating to have them parading around our front lawn?"

"Parading?" Dee said. "Titillating?"

Stewart twirled one of the strips enticingly in front of him and spoke huskily.

"Hey, sailor, how long will you be in Shanghai?"

"Stewart!" Dee shook her head, brushed past him, and walked across the hall to the bathroom.

"Well, you find something less erotic to tie back the rose bushes and we will use that," she said from behind the bathroom door.

"Erotic, that's a modern word," Stewart mumbled, then called louder, "I will. I'm going to find some good old-fashioned rags made from a discarded T-shirt or a sexless pair of socks. That is what this calls for—good ol' rags. That's a good name for a dog, too. 'Hey, Rags, come here boy. That's a good boy. Bit any sailors today?'"

He began clattering around the house, looking for rags

and still mumbling.

"What if the TV antenna got blown off the roof? What would Dee suggest? Strapping it down with one of her brassieres?"

Stewart walked to the front door and entertained a quick mental image of the door laden with his various modes of locks. He savored the thought for a moment and then opened the door, continuing to hold forth as he walked across the lawn.

"I can just imagine the neighbors now. 'Hey, Stewart, the storm blew a hole in our roof last night. Does Dee have a pair of panties we can use to patch it? A thong might work in a pinch.'"

He walked around the corner of the house and found Charlene standing with her shoulders drooped and her arms folded across her abdomen. The children played in a loose circle around her.

"Ah, Charlene," he said. "Don't you think you could knit something like these?"

"Stockings?" Charlene asked.

"Yes," Stewart said.

"They wouldn't be very comfortable."

"No, not to wear. Dee wanted to use these to tie the rose bushes back, but I think you will agree that these are not very appropriate."

Charlene took one of the nylon strips and held them in her hand.

"Sure," she said. "You know, if Dee is just going to throw

these away, I could use them to put my gladiola bulbs in and hang them from the front porch."

Stewart swiped the strip from her hand.

"No, we are going to donate these to local schoolchildren. Turns out they make wonderful book straps."

Charlene looked past him.

"Who's that?"

Stewart turned and saw a brown van parked in the driveway. His mind raced to match the color and form to his memory. Then the passenger door opened, and Amy hopped out and came running toward him. She flattened her face against his chest and wrapped her arms around him.

"Dad had to come to New Orleans for business. He wanted to call first, but we wanted to surprise you."

She broke away from Stewart and hugged Charlene—a board-stiff Charlene, who flushed exceedingly and kept her arms folded. Amy was not much taller than when she had left but her figure had grown and bulged into a chubby, cute form. A lone long pimple, bright red, stood out on her chin, paling, and then blossoming with her active smile.

"And this is Karmen," Amy said.

She pulled a young man forward by his wrist. He was dressed in dark, baggy clothing. His equally dark hair was a fashionable mess. Yet, he was well-mannered to a scripted fault.

"How do you do, sir?" he said. "Amy has told me so much about you. I very much look forward to getting to know you very much better."

Stewart nodded. Well, the young man could certainly follow directions, he thought.

"Your dad?" Stewart said, walking toward to the van.

He heard Amy's voice behind him as he came closer and closer to the van.

"No, he's back at the hotel. He said he'd come see y'all tomorrow evening. So, Charlene. How have you been? This is my friend, Karmen. Karmen, Charlene, and this is ... let me see if I can remember—Darren, David, Dwight ..."

Tim stepped out of one of the van's rear double doors. He held a package in his arms wrapped in the Sunday color comics.

"For me?" Stewart asked.

Tim looked up, surprised.

"Oh ... hey. Ah, no. Amy got it for Karmen's birthday. I'm supposed to hide it."

"What do you think of this Karmen guy," Stewart said. "Isn't that a girl's name?"

"Boy and girl name, I think," Tim said. "I don't know. He seems like a nice guy, but I don't think he's good enough for Amy. It makes me angry that he's so nice because I'd really like to hate him, but I can't since he's so nice. And that makes me hate him even more. You know what I'm saying."

Stewart closed his eyes in affirmation.

"Nice guys are almost impossible not to hate."

"Exactly," Tim said.

"And, of course, if he ever does anything to hurt her, you will beat him to the point of death then drive him over here and let me finish the job."

"That's a promise," Tim said.

"Very thoughtful of you," Stewart said. "It's a long drive, but we could split the gas. In the meantime, put that thing in a bag and we'll hide it upstairs behind our winter clothes. By the way, how was the drive from San Diego?"

"As wicked and as long as it sounds," Tim said.

They walked toward the front steps of the house.

"What did she get him, anyway?"

Tim shrugged.

"Pants, I think."

Stewart stopped suddenly.

"What do you have on your shirt, there?" he asked.

Tim put his hands up in front of him.

"Yeah, right," he said.

"No seriously," Stewart said. He put his hand between Tim's guard and pulled a piece of what looked to be yarn from his shirt. He balled it between his fingers and let it float away in the air.

"It must be from the carpeting in the van," Stewart said.

"Yeah. Hey, there's a little on you, too," Tim said.

Stewart pressed his chin against his chest.

"Where?"

Tim pointed to an area in the center of Stewart's shirt and then flicked Stewart's nose upward. He laughed nervously, put his hands up in a defensive posture and backed away.

Stewart acknowledged his advantage with a slight tilt of his head.

"Dad will fall for that a hundred times a day," Tim said. "You would think they'd have taught him that in the Navy."

"Budget cuts," Stewart said. "By the way, who do you like living with better—him or me?"

"Him," Tim said, immediately.

Stewart opened the front door and gestured with his hand for Tim to enter first.

"I can't blame you," he said, "But you could have paused for half a beat before answering that question."

"Hey, but I came back to see you, didn't I?" Tim said. "I mean, Amy could have driven herself. What are you doing with those stockings?"

Stewart looked at the strips he was still holding and then gave them to Tim.

"They're for Karmen," he said. "Make sure he gets them."

Dee was putting drinks and food on the table when they walked in. Fresh tears arose immediately in her already reddened eyes at the sight of Tim.

"Look at him. He's a man," she said.

She set the plate she was holding down on the table and walked toward him. She put her hands on his cheek for a long moment. Then ran them along his shoulders and down his arms. Tim flushed and smiled uneasily. He leaned forward and kissed Dee on the cheek.

"Dad's at the hotel. He said he'd come by tomorrow, if that's okay."

Dee studied his face as he spoke, heard the deepening lilt of his voice and a new set of tears came to her eyes.

Amy came dashing down the hall.

"You should see the rooms," she said. "They look like little cubby holes. They are so small and cute."

Karmen followed at her heels. He gave a vacant, nervous smile and looked about the house for some space that he might fit into. To him the whole place was a doll house in which he did not belong.

"You mind if I look at my old room?" Tim asked.

Dee had tilted her head back slightly, embarrassed by her tears now and trying to stifle any more.

"Of course, look through the whole house and yard if you want. Make yourself—I . . ." she stopped and tilted her head again.

Charlene and the children had come into the house now. The area in which they stood, a hallway just off the kitchen, had become very crowded, close, and noisy. Amy was trying to get Hope to leave her mother and come to her. Darren and David, wearing baseball gloves and caps and carrying identical bats, were bugging Karmen to play baseball. Dwight was heading for the pots and pans in the row of low cabinets beneath the sink.

Dee dabbed her eyes with the corner of a dish towel.

"I'm sorry," she said. "It's just that seeing them again brought back so much to me. So much that I miss."

"Well, yes, I know," Stewart said, awkwardly.

"What's in the bag?" Dee asked.

"A pair of pants, I believe, for Karmen's birthday. I'm going to go hide it. Oh, and I want those two seated at opposite poles from one another for lunch," Stewart said.

By the time everyone had settled down to eat, Wade had come in from his new job. He was painting the house of a friend of Dee's parents. He had completed the scraping and had applied fresh paint to about a quarter of the house. Updates on the job were a staple at dinner time.

"Home early today," Stewart said.

"Yeah, it started clouding up and Mrs. Gomez said since it's Saturday, I might want to call it a day. Better than painting a side and having the rain ruin it," Wade said.

Stewart was looking at him as the activity of bowls being passed and plates being heaped went on about him.

"You can call her," Wade said, defensively.

"Did I say anything?" Stewart asked the guests at the table. He glanced out the window opposite the table. He had to block his eyes from the sun.

"I can see those thunderheads brewing now," Stewart said. "My corns will start shrieking any minute."

"Come on," Dee said. "Stewart, pass the rice, will you?"

Stewart picked up the bowl of rice and handed it down the table.

"Just pray the levee holds," he said.

"So, does your dad miss the Navy?" Wade asked Tim and Amy.

"I don't think so," Tim said.

"He was tired of traveling around so much," Amy added. "I think he was ready to settle down and have a place called home."

"I always wanted to be in the Navy," Wade said wistfully. His face was flecked with paint, and he reeked of mineral spirits.

"Why didn't you join?" Amy asked.

"Bum back," Stewart, Dee, and Charlene answered in unison.

Wade nodded. He chewed a piece of bread, absently.

"Country's loss," Stewart said.

"So, Karmen, what do you do?" Stewart asked, suddenly.

Karmen looked up from his plate as the activity at the table abruptly ceased. Even the children were waiting for an answer.

"He goes to school with me," Amy answered.

"Amy, honey, I asked Karmen. You must let him answer for himself," Stewart said.

"I, uh, go to high school," Karmen said. "With Amy."

Tim was seated next to Stewart. His lips were curled around a mouth of food in a barely suppressed grin.

"Just the two of you, alone, in the whole school," Tim said. "How nice."

Amy glared at him, and Karmen made a futile attempt to return to his food.

"What do you plan to do when you graduate from high school?" Stewart asked.

"He's going—" Amy began and then fell silent.

"He's going —" Karmen said and stopped. He rolled his eyes at his own fumbling and then began again, bravely. "I'm going to college. Maybe USC. I hope to get my undergraduate degree there and then go to law school out of state. Maybe even here at Tulane. I hear they have an excellent law school."

A rush of approval was released from the table.

"Well, that's just wonderful," Dee said. "I'm sure you'll do just fine."

"That's where the beans are," Wade said, sagaciously. "I always wanted to go to law school."

"Bum back," Stewart said.

"My daddy's got a friend that's a lawyer," Charlene said. "You should see the size of their home. And that's just their summer home."

Darren raised a spoon towards Karmen.

"Perry Mason," he said.

Everyone at the table laughed. Nearly everyone.

"He watches Perry Mason on television," Wade explained. "That's his favorite show. You like Perry Mason, huh, Darren? Karmen's going to be a Perry Mason. The next Perry Mason."

A lawyer, Stewart thought, and leaned close to Tim.

"I knew I didn't like him," he said.

Tim nodded appreciatively.

When all the food had been passed, the table chatter gave way to concentrated eating. Stewart and Tim settled their elbows at the same corner of the table at the same moment. The two arms brushed together and then rested ever so slightly against the other.

"Sorry," Tim said.

"Sorry," Stewart said.

But neither moved their arm.

Chapter 30

Wade's hands shook as they reached out to grasp the ladder. The morning sun heated the top of his uncovered head and demanded a payment of sweat which began at his hairline and ran, in a glistening sheet, down the length of his face. He climbed the ladder until he was window level against the raised home. He stepped timidly from the ladder onto the scaffolding he had erected, placing one foot in the middle of the heavy timber and following with the other only after he had as secure a grip as possible, given the circumstances, on the metal frame. Each movement was accompanied with the heaviness of a fresh and active hangover. He flattened his buttocks against the board in front of the section of wall where the previous day's strokes ended. He took a stiff paintbrush in one hand, looked at the wall, and then placed the brush back on the unopened can. He sucked in his lower lip. A tear fell out the corner of both eyes and was lost among the sweat sheen covering his face. He brushed the tears away with his wrists but two more immediately fell in their place. He looked at the wall scornfully, picked the can of paint off the board next to him, and threw it as hard as he could against the wall. It bounced off, clipped the metal frame of the scaffolding, and then dug into the ground below, its contents gurgling grotesquely from the fractured seal.

Wade jumped onto the crossbar of the scaffolding and dropped to the ground. He staggered to a tree and began vomiting. His sides constricted and heaved with each retch. When he finished, the world looked as if he were viewing it from underwater. The Buick floated in a bubble of soft focus in the Gomezs' driveway. He lunged toward the car and fell in behind the wheel. He turned over the motor, threw the car in gear, and screeched out of the driveway.

Twenty minutes later he sat in the sun against the back wall of Trader's Lounge. Hours later he was still there, looking up at the diminishing sun with closed, suffering eyes. His Adam's apple shifted up and down, bulging through his taut neckline. A half-empty bottle of wine was stuck between his legs. Someone kicked his foot. Wade opened his eyes in protest and leveled his head. It was Ted, who gestured to the bottle between Wade's legs.

"Mind?" he asked.

Wade waved his hand weakly. The old man picked up the bottle and turned it happily into his mouth.

"Here to stay this time?" Ted asked in the gasp that

came at the end of his long swig.

"I just needed to do some thinking," Wade said.

The old man looked at the wine bottle.

"Looks like you done some pretty good thinking before I come."

Wade closed his eyes again.

"You like me?" Ted asked.

Wade opened his eyes and grinned.

"I don't even know your name," he said.

"I told you it a hundred times. At least I think I did, but maybe not. Maybe we never even met before or maybe we best of friends. It's a wonder life when you step out of the way for good and let everyone just glide by. Wonder life. Glide by."

The old man wiggled his fingers in the air, tipped the bottle and took another long drink.

"You like to be like me?" he asked.

Wade grinned again and shook his head.

"You well on your way. People don't think the old man knows. They don't think he sees that he's different from other people; that he's at the bottom of the heap. But he knows. Difference is, he don't care."

"Sometimes I don't think I care either," Wade said.

"Ah, you still care," the old man said. "I hear you crying for that woman of yours and mumbling after all them children. But you keep like you're going and soon you won't care a nickel for the whole world. You won't mumble anyone's name again. But you'll know. That's what keeps you drinking, the knowing."

Ted paused for a moment and then burst into loud laughter. He brushed away the two points of hair at the corner of his mouth that had again escaped the restraint of his bandana.

"Listen to the philosophy this evening" he howled. "Ho-Ho-Ho-Ho. Ah-Ah-Ah."

Wade started suddenly.

"Evening?" he said. "What time is it?"

"It's late," the old man said in baleful tones. "Later than you think." He raised the bottle merrily to his mouth.

Wade stood up quickly. He scurried to the Buick and leaned through the open window. He tapped the plastic covering of the clock that was built into the instrument panel. It had stopped at nine o'clock.

"Time," Wade said.

He ran along the sidewalk until he was in front of Trader's.

"Time?" he asked a passerby.

The man squinted at his watch.

"It's a quarter of."

"A quarter of what?" Wade asked.

"A quarter of the hour," the man said, impatiently.

"Of what hour?"

"Five!" the man shouted.

Wade dashed into Trader's.

"Unless you are here to pay your tab, get out," an angry voice said. It was the owner.

The brightness of the sun had contracted Wade's pupils

so that the barroom now stood in almost complete darkness.

"I mean it, buddy," the owner said.

Wade reached into his pocket and felt the curve of a quarter nestled at its bottom.

"One phone call," he said. He dove into the darkness and clattered into a wooden and glass phone booth. When he shut the booth, a small light came on and returned a tiny part of the world to his eyes. He slipped the coin into the payphone and pressed the buttons, impatiently. It rang three times before someone answered.

"Charlene?" Wade said. "It's not important where I am. I know. I was sick."

Wade looked up at the light as the voice on the other end filled the earpiece.

"I was sick," Wade pleaded. "I couldn't paint. I'll get back on the job in the morning. What's it matter?"

He paused.

"I'm at Trader's Okay? All right? Now, listen. Today is the drawing for the lottery. You have to remember to watch. It's coming on in about ten minutes."

There was a sound at the door of the phone booth. Wade looked up and saw an angry palm slap against the glass of the door.

"Come on, you bum. I don't get no money for you tying up the line."

The voice was muffled by the closed door but still

sounded fierce. Wade bent his foot against the door, blocking entry.

"It's important that you watch it," Wade said into the phone. "I've always believed that you brought me luck. I think I picked good numbers this time."

"Block my door, huh?" the owner yelled. "I'll call the police. They'll lock you up for vagrancy. They'll lock you up for not paying your tab."

"You're the only hope I have," Wade said finally. "Please, just watch. Just watch and hope. Okay. . . . Yes, yes. I'm coming home. Yes. Now? Well, soon. Soon. I promise. I promise. Yes. Soon. Goodbye."

Wade returned the receiver to its cradle and moved his foot from the door. Four hands reached into the booth and took hold of him. He was dragged to the door and heaved toward the sidewalk. He landed squarely inside a sturdy cardboard box in which a new cooler had been delivered that afternoon. The box was filled with Styrofoam packing beans which covered Wade like a bubble bath.

Wade watched from the box as the imposing figure of the owner walked toward him. He wished Marie were here to calm him down. But instead, several men appeared behind the owner and brought him back toward the door.

"He ain't worth it. They'll come and arrest you. You'll lose your business," one man pleaded with him, as hands grappled to restrain him.

The owner managed to raise an arm against the

restriction of his fellows.

"Don't you ever come in here again," he said. "Don't you ever show your face around here, you drunk. Stay off my sidewalk. Get out of my garbage."

The men had to exert more force to restrain him now that he had found a new affront.

"You hear me? Get out of my garbage. You're not good enough to be in my garbage. Stay out of my trash."

The men pulled the owner back towards the building. Wade watched them disappear through the door. Slowly, he sank deeper and deeper into the box until the Styrofoam eggs covered him completely.

Chapter 31

Stewart was at work and Tim, Amy, and Karmen were not due for a return visit until later that evening when they promised to bring their dad. Dee had the house completely to herself but still she felt crowded upon, watched, and scrutinized, as she knelt before the low table at the back of closet. All the necessary steps had been taken. All that was left to do was for her to dip the white strip of chemically treated paper into the three-inch-high container resting on the table. If the paper stayed the same color, she could put away the preparations for another month, store her hopes for another day. If the paper changed to a dark blue . . .

Dee closed her eyes. She held the strip of paper between thumb and forefinger and tried to settle her breathing. She lowered the paper in the direction of the container. She would hold it there for ten minutes, willfully keeping her eyes closed the whole time. With a minute to go, she checked her watch. She kept her eye trained on the second hand as it swept around the circumference of the watch. When the hand completed its revolution, she pulled the strip up and forced herself to look at the results. Her face immediately fell in complete disappointment.

The paper retained its original color. In fact, it had not even been stained slightly from its immersion in her urine. In fact, it was bone dry. In fact, she had missed the container completely and had held the paper against the top of the table and waited and prayed for ten minutes.

"Well, the table is not pregnant," Dee said.

This was ridiculous, she told herself. Keep your eyes open this time. Quit shaking.

Charlene dropped the portable phone to the floor in disgust. Holding Hope against her belly, she went to the bar and lifted a gallon of vodka from the shelf. Beneath the vodka lay the lottery ticket for that day's drawing.

"You were sick?" Charlene said. "Well, I'm sick, too."

Even in her great disgust, the level and tone of her voice did not change perceptibly. She switched on the television and took a seat in a wicker rocker opposite it. She laid the ticket on the bed. She swung Hope onto her knee. The familiar commercials that preceded *Lotto Luck* began to flash onto the screen. Charlene could not believe she had bothered Dee to take her to the Gomezs' house so she could bring Wade's lunch to him and he was not even there. A busted can of paint dripping into the soil was the only evidence he had been there at all that day.

What did Dee think of him? Of her? What would Mrs. Gomez say when she came home? What would Stewart think? What would they do if Wade lost this job, too? Charlene wondered if he ever asked himself any of these questions. Or was that her lot? To ask and answer for him. To have his babies and cook his dinner and to play lady luck for him by watching his stupid *Lotto Luck*.

Luck. Wade ran into some hard luck, that was for sure, but he certainly manufactured enough of his own trouble.

Peter Barber appeared on the screen before an oversized Lotto form.

"Good evening and welcome to *Lotto Luck*," he said. "Where just a few minutes can change a life forever. My name is Pete Barber and, if you've been watching *Lotto Luck* regularly, you know that our possible winnings for this week's drawing have accumulated to an amazing, record-breaking $115 million."

He paused to let the sum make an impression on the viewing audience.

"Yes, I did say million. Ha. Ha. Now that sum could be won by one person or equally divided among several winners. But, in any case, it is indeed a large sum and I know I'm excited about the prospect of having a winner today. So, I want you to help me welcome our guest for today's drawing . . ."

Charlene suddenly scooped the ticket up in one hand and crumbled it in her fist. She threw the wadded ticket at the television.

"Watch your own *Lotto Luck,* why don't you?" she said.

The ticket, too light to travel very far, floated and landed on the bed covering. Charlene set Hope down on the bed and began looking for her shoes. She was determined to not be around when the winning numbers were called. Darren and David were playing at a neighbor's house. She could put Hope and Dwight in a stroller and go visit Dee for a little while.

"So, you're a model for a surfing company on the West Coast. Is that correct, Susan?" the announcer was saying.

Charlene suddenly stopped as she went to tie one of Hope's shoes. Her nose crinkled in mild disgust.

"Honey, not again," she said. She walked through one of the quilts and came back with a fresh disposable diaper and powder.

"Now, as a model, I'm sure you know all about taking risks," Peter said.

"Definitely," Susan said. "Whenever you're modeling a new line, you're always out on the edge yourself, really trying to sell yourself as part of the fashion concept."

"Indeed," Peter Barber said. "Sounds exciting."

"Oh, it is," Susan said. "The element of risk is what really keeps it exciting and, of course, the people you have an opportunity to work with are all very, really, special."

"Risk and excitement are what we're all about here at *Lotto Luck*," Peter Barber said. "So, if you're ready, I know I'm ready and the folks at home are ready, why don't you press our number selector and let's see if we can't have a winner."

Hope began to kick in protest and utter sharp cries. Charlene struggled to keep her on top of the diaper she had placed under her.

"Hope, behave," she said.

One of her kicks knocked over the open container of baby powder. It fell off the bed and rolled onto the floor, leaving a trail of powder in its wake.

"Hope!" Charlene said. She leaned over to pick up the container.

"And there are the winning numbers for today's lottery. 15, 40, 7, 3, 86, 2," Peter Barber said.

Charlene's head jerked over the bed instantly. No. They just sound similar, like all of them sound similar when you've tried for so long. She remembered Wade fretting over the numbers like he always did and repeating them over and over again. No. They just sounded familiar like they always did. But why did these sound so very familiar this time?

"15, 40, 7, 3, 86, 2," Peter Barber repeated. "Now, remember if these six numbers appear on your ticket, in any sequence, you have twenty . . ."

Charlene looked at the crumbled stub on the bedsheet. The end of the ticket was twisted so that only three of its numbers showed—15, 40, 7. Charlene placed both hands against her mouth. She looked back at the screen. She took one hand from her mouth and placed it on the bed beside the ticket. Her forefinger slipped under the fold she had crumpled in anger and lifted its paper hatch, slowly revealing the remaining numbers.

Dee had her eyes closed again, but she was certain the paper had made contact this time. Hadn't she, indeed, heard a minute lapping and felt the soundless draw of the paper fibers? She had just checked her watch and knew that only ten seconds remained until the results would be ready. She counted to ten, then to fifteen just to be sure. Still, she did not bring her hand up or open her eyes. This was ridiculous, she knew. This was so silly. If Stewart or anyone could see her behind the curtain of clothing, she would die with shame. She could not stop shaking. Finally, she brought her trembling hand up and opened her eyes. The paper was a deep, dark blue. The bluest blue Dee had ever seen.

"Charlene!" Dee cried. In the same instant she heard a matching cry come from the addition.

"Dee!"

Dee shot up and hit her head hard on the shelf above her. She slapped the shelf in retaliation and, holding her head, threaded her way through the clothes. She stomped down the hall like a schoolboy and burst through the back screen door.

"Charlene!" she yelled.

Charlene was fumbling with the handle of the door that led out of the addition. She had locked and unlocked it twice. Finally, she opened the door and came out into the backyard, holding a crying and half-naked Hope under one arm.

"You know?" Charlene said.

"Yes, yes, yes!" Dee said.

They ran towards each other and gave a full embrace. Hope wailed loudly as she was crushed between the two joining bodies. Tears streamed down the faces of all three.

"Sweetheart, I'm so happy," Dee said breathlessly. "I've never felt so happy. Stewart is going to cry. I know he is. He is just going to forget everything he knows and is and is just going to break down and cry."

"Wade's going to be so proud," Charlene said. "Nothing like this has ever happened to him before and he's worked so hard at it too. I know Stewart has always done his job, but to Wade it was his job too. He wanted this so badly."

Dee gave her a look that contained the residue of her tears, a slight, stunned smile, and a wrinkled forehead of newfound consternation.

"Sweetheart, you need to settle down," Dee said, taking Charlene by the hand and leading her to one of the lawn chairs. Hope instinctively climbed upon her lap. "Here, just sit down and try to calm yourself. I had no idea you'd be this excited."

Charlene was crying unabashedly now. She held the child limply in her arms.

"Oh, but you don't know how long I've waited for this day. How hard I've worked for it, too. It may have looked like I was just sitting around, but it was work for me, too. And, now, everyone is going to say what a lucky, wise and wonderful couple—Charlene and Wade."

Dee snapped her fist against her hips.

"It's ours. Mine and Stewart's. Nobody else gets any credit."

Charlene sniffed loudly and came to half-composure.

"Oh, Dee, let's not argue. Of course, we owe you and Stewart so much. Of course, you can have half of it, or even more, if you'd like. We only need a little bit."

Dee's eyes narrowed and her brow plunged into an angry "V" at the top of her nose.

"Are you crazy? Have you been taking drugs?"

"I feel like I have been," Charlene said. "When I saw those numbers on the screen, it was like I was dreaming—I just couldn't believe it. I had to hold up the ticket right against the glass of the screen and make sure it was real. My heart was pounding so fast, I thought I would catch a heart attack. I thought, Wouldn't this be great? Win all that money and then die of a heart attack before you can claim it."

Dee gripped the arms of the lawn chair and faced Charlene directly.

"You won the lottery?"

"I know," Charlene said, "Keep saying it. It sounds so

sweet. $115 million. Isn't that a sweet number?"

Dee released her grip from the chair and clapped her hands.

"Charlene, I'm pregnant. I just found out using that home testing kit we bought at the grocery the other day."

"Pregnant?" Charlene said, breathlessly.

She held out weak arms toward Dee and new tears came forth. Dee fell into her arms.

"That's what I meant, by it being all mine and Stewart's," Dee said.

"That's what I meant by saying y'all could take half," Charlene said.

She stood and joined hands with Dee. They both began dancing in a circle.

"This has got to be the happiest day anybody ever had," Charlene said.

"One hundred and fifteen million and a baby," Dee said. "Should we tell Wade and Stewart before we go to the mall?"

Naked Hope twirled in the grass between them, lifting her arms. Dee and Charlene broke their hold to include her.

"I've got so much to do," Charlene said. "I've got to go look at that ticket again. I've got to get this baby dressed. I've got to make some phone calls. How do you make a long-distance call and charge it to yourself?"

Dee threw her head back and laughed.

"I can show you. It's easier than charging it to someone else."

Chapter 32

Stewart steered the Ranger onto the ribbon strips of the driveway slowly, wearily. He emitted a long low sigh through slack lips and, after a moment's reflection, exited the vehicle. In one hand has his empty water jug, its white top grimed permanently with the ink of days spent handling other people's mail. Draped over one shoulder was a blue, vinyl raincoat that had ill-served him during that afternoon's rainstorm. He walked up the front steps and pulled the door handle of the half-glass, half-screen door that they had installed last hurricane season. It was locked, which made perfect sense, but, at the moment, seemed like one more obstacle between him and home. He placed the jug on the steps, reached deep into his pants pocket and pulled out a wedge of keys. He found one slender steel bar, the same size and shape as a sardine can opener. He inserted the key into the hole.

"Silly fake key," he muttered, twisting the bar into the lock. "Stupid cheap key for overpriced, ignorant door."

He jiggled the key in the lock a number of times and, finally, the door opened. As he entered the house, the raincoat slipped from his shoulder and fell between the screen door and the jamb. The trapped coat pulled him backwards as he tried to move farther into the house. After several futile attempts to loosen the coat from the door's grip, he relented and moved back to open the door. Once released, he gathered the coat on his arm, closed the door again, and then leaned down to pick up his water jug. His hand opened and closed around dead air near the surface of the floor.

"Outside," he muttered.

He opened the screen door and heard the water jug bounce down the steps. It landed between the fronds of the sago palm, which he had planted for the sole purpose of producing foliage for Palm Sunday Masses, and a flourishing yucca. He went down the steps and stood between the two plants. He pricked his hands against the spiked edge of the palm fronds as he reached to retrieve the jug and then backed into the spear of the yucca.

"Ahhh, knives," he said, in private misery. "Et tu, cacti?"

He walked back onto the steps and tried the door. It was locked. He patted his pockets and then visualized his wedge of keys sitting on the tall corner table just inside the door where he always placed them to avoid leaving them and locking himself out.

"Dee. Practical assistance, needed," he called knocking

on the door. "Come meet me and help me, my helpmeet."

"Stewart," Dee sang merrily on the opposite side of the door. "Oh, Stewart!"

The lock clicked loudly against the door's metal frame and swung open widely, nearly sweeping him back into the garden. He sidestepped the door and entered the foyer where Dee encircled him in her arms and kissed his lips, his forehead, and neck.

"Dee, please. It is not even dusk. Plus, I have been punctured by that vindictive sago and lanced through by the Mexican assassin you planted out there. It is now the size of a sequoia, by the way. Are there any holes in me? Look, will you?"

"Stewart, you are going to be so happy in just a few seconds," Dee said.

Stewart had turned with his back to her.

"The entry wounds should be somewhere in the scapular area," he said pointing to his back. "Don't remove any vegetative antler you see lodged in my skin; I might bleed out."

Dee placed her hands on his shoulders and turned him around.

"Stewart, listen," she said.

She looked full into his face and felt such a rush of love for him and the oblivious, slightly annoyed, and questioning expression he gave her that she fell to kissing him again and again. Stewart pulled back.

"Wade's been abducted?" he asked hopefully.

"Stewart you must look further and deeper. Why look at the candle when the sun is blazing on you."

"My wife—the fourteenth Dalai Lama," Stewart said.

She kissed him again.

"Your wife—the mother of your child," Dee said. "And your brother, who has not been abducted but won the lottery and is a multi-multi-multi-millionaire. The richest person we will ever know."

Stewart stepped back and looked at her. He took another step back and rattled against the corner table. His face was completely drained of color except for two rouge reservoirs high along his cheekbones.

"A baby?" he asked. He held both hands in front of him in a diminutive gesture.

Dees eyes brimmed with tears that fell down her face as she nodded.

"I just didn't think," Stewart said weakly. "I just didn't believe we could, ever. I mean the doctors."

The rims of his own eyes bulged with soft emotion.

"I just . . . and Wade won himself a million dollars."

"One hundred and fifteen million dollars," Dee said. "It's a world record."

"A record," Stewart said. "I just didn't believe. Really, I didn't. That bum found one hundred and fifteen, did you say, one hundred and fifteen *million* dollars, just sitting on someone's lost driver's license, or a gum wrapper, or a streetcar, and we found a baby just being together like we always have been."

The tears Dee had predicted now came, tracing two disciplined lines down the sides of his face.

"Excuse me," someone said through the screen door. Stewart looked and saw the face of a man he had seen a thousand times before but could not immediately place. The man's gray hair was scrupulously coifed with a wide, pink part running on the left side of his scalp. His face appeared slightly powdered, and he wore a perfectly fitted suit.

"Alex Hunter," Dee said.

The man looked down, slightly embarrassed.

"Yes, ma'am. We're with Channel 8—the news watcher. We were looking for the winner of the lottery. I'm afraid the news is out. I hope I have the address correct. Is this the home of the winner?"

Behind Alex Hunter was a man dressed in jeans and a striped polo shirt. He held a large television camera against his shoulder and looked through its viewer constantly, as if it were his only eye to the world.

"Yes," Stewart said. "This is the home of the winner."

Chapter 33

They chose the yucca plant as the backdrop. Wade stood in front of it and Alex Hunter stood next to him, continually looking at the camera and then back at Wade. A technician and a light man scrambled behind the stationary camera man. In the street behind them was the station's satellite truck, its dish angled imploringly at the evening sky.

"Okay, I think we can go with that voice level," the technician said, into a headset mic. "Angle those lights just a wee bit tighter. Perfect. Yes, we are ready to go live in just . . . "

"Whose arm is that in the upper right quadrant of my shot?" the camera operator said.

That would be Stewart's arm. He was standing on the top step leaning across the railing at an unwise angle with a can of paint in one hand and a brush in the other. The arm of the hand that held the brush was stretched to a breaking point as it ached to reach the weatherboards directly behind Wade. His strokes quickened at the sound of the man's voice.

"Sorry," he called back and stepped off the steps and onto the front lawn. "Should have taken care of that bare spot last spring. Rains."

He pointed with the brush and spoke to the technician.

"Now, since Wade is left-handed, shouldn't he and Alex shift places?"

Alex, the technician, and Wade looked at him in silence. Even the cameraman took his eye away from the viewer and stared at him. Only Wade was smiling. So far, this guy had hosed down the steps, fertilized the lawn around Alex and the lottery winner, scrubbed a window that wasn't even going to be in the shot, commented on the warp and woof of Alex's coat and waxed the leaves of that stupid yucca plant that had poked Alex. Twice.

"Just a loyal viewer's suggestion," Stewart said to the staring faces. "Proceed. Go on. Action."

"Okay, we are ready to go live," the technician said. "If we could have a little quiet please."

An expanding knot of neighbors were gathering along the sidewalk standing just outside the arc of light that illumined the area around Wade.

"Yes, let's have quiet," Stewart commanded the silent crowd. "Just pipe down and we can get a good production out of this."

Dee reached out of the darkness and pulled Stewart next to her.

"What?" he said.

"Shhh," Dee said and pointed at the set. Once again, all faces were turned towards him.

"More paint?" Stewart asked, offering the brush.

Alex Hunter swished his microphone cord to one side, touched his tie where it was knotted and began speaking.

"This morning Wade Terry awoke with a special feeling, a hunch if you will, that something good was about to happen. This evening, the thirty-three-year-old laborer learned he was a millionaire, many times over . . ."

Stewart looked at his neighbors.

"Alex is really network material don't you think? If anything were to ever happen to David Brinkley, heaven forbid, you're looking at his replacement."

Dee elbowed him into silence.

Wade had showered and shaved before the interview and looked bright and expanded under the lights.

"When I went to work, I just kept thinking about the lottery the whole time and every time I thought about it, I felt good," Wade said.

"And you're basically a subcontractor, right?" Alex said.

"Yeah, well, I do a little of this and a little of that," Wade laughed.

"Very little of both, actually," Stewart said.

Dee pinched him.

"Now, are you going to tell us how you arrived at the winning numbers or are you going to keep it a secret?" Alex asked.

"The human touch," Stewart told the neighbors. "That's

what makes them the news watchers of the Greater New Orleans Area."

"Stewart, please," Dee whispered.

Hope squirmed in Charlene's arms and let out a soft coo.

"Shhh!" Stewart said, harshly.

Dwight moved toward Stewart's legs awkwardly, grabbed onto his trousers to keep from falling and stuck a finger to his lips.

"Shhh!" he mimicked.

"Numbers are funny things," Wade was telling Alex. "I arrived at my winning numbers by taking my ranking on the postal exam, which I had totally blown, and combining it with the birthdate of my youngest boy Dwight."

Dwight laughed with both hands against his face at the mention of his name.

"It was like the worst and best parts of my life all smashed up together," Wade said. "I guess that's what winning is all about."

Alex went to say something and then stopped.

"Well put," he said, admiringly. "I think we will leave it at that. Mr. Terry, I know you have a lot of celebrating to do with your family and friends gathered here, so we'll let you get back to that."

The camera brought Alex's face close up to the viewing screen and Wade receded into the background.

"I'm Alex Hunter with America's newest multi-millionaire reporting live from New Orleans's Navarre neighborhood for Channel 8, the news watcher of southern Louisiana."

Alex relaxed his stance, coiled the microphone cord and held it loosely in one hand. He shook Wade's hand as the crew began to strike the lights. The neighbors moved as a body across the lawn and began congratulating Wade. It was not long before more news people with more cameras and lights showed up and the neighbors were pushed back to the edge of the sidewalk.

Wade repeated his story over and over again, showing an unexpected degree of polish and charm and igniting an easy rapport with each successive reporter. He was big news. On the last taping of the night, Stewart managed to insert the standing banner of the Knights of Columbus, St. Andrew's Council, 3685 behind Wade. He also added a layer of pea gravel around the yucca plant while muttering various imprecations regarding its naked aggression. It was close to midnight when the last news van pulled away from the curb. Most of the neighbors had drifted away during the evening. Charlene sat drowsing on the hood of the Buick, the children spread around her on the hood in comfortless and precarious slumber. Dee sat on the strip of driveway itself, her back braced against the rear wheel of the Buick, her knees pulled up with her arms and head resting against them.

Stewart waved to the departing media, bid a lingering neighbor goodnight, and came up the lawn towards Wade. He was sitting on the top step, rubbing his cheek with his hands and inspecting them under the porchlight.

"That second lady put powder on me," Wade said. "Do I look like a clown?"

Stewart took a triumphant perch on the step below Wade.

"You look like a million bucks," he said.

"A hundred and fifteen million."

"One hundred and fifteen million," Stewart corrected and shook his head. "You did it. You . . . just did it. Hoo boy. I had more faith in the tooth fairy than I did in you, but you did it."

"The lottery committee man said the first check will arrive before the end of the month, if I want to take it in installments. They want to fly me up to New York for some kind of ceremonial signing. I didn't know I was going to break a record. I just played every week. I never been to New York."

Stewart waved a hand forward.

"It's probably not as bad as they say," Stewart said. "A few more pollutants and lunatics than our fair city, most likely."

"Imagine the change and how fast it happened," Wade said.

"Yes, imagine all that change," Stewart said.

"Hey, congratulations on the baby. I know y'all put your time in on that one," Wade said.

Stewart smiled.

"Thanks."

"So, what are you going to do with your half? I always said you had half of it coming to you," Wade said.

Stewart shifted his position and his elbow tapped something on the step above him that made a distinctive ring. Wade reached behind Stewart and brought forth a brown paper bag. He lifted a green wet bottle out of the bag.

"Champagne," he said. "Mrs. Dugas brought it over and told me she had always been in love with me."

He lowered the bottle back into the bag and set it between his feet.

"So, come on. What are you going to do with your half?"

"I am going to thank you sincerely and give it back to you," Stewart said.

"Give it back to me? What for? It's yours," Wade said, heatedly.

"No, it's not Wade. It's yours. You earned that money by the gamble you were willing to take. If it were up to me, you would never have spent one penny on those crazy numbers you found—and then where would you be?"

"But if it wasn't for you, where would Charlene and me be?" Wade asked. "How would I have fed my kids?"

"True," Stewart said. "That's why I don't feel too brash asking you for a favor."

"What? You name it," Wade said. "I'll give you a million dollars right now. That's the least I can do. I could leave a million dollars as a tip for a stranger."

Stewart held up his hand.

"I don't need a million dollars," Stewart said. "I just need enough to start over again—to start fresh. You know I have some education—two years shy of a degree, but it seems like the only thing I use my knowledge for is to ridicule other people. Sometimes, they don't even know I am ridiculing them because I will make some reference to something they don't know. It's an awful habit really but one I am very unlikely to quit. I enjoy doing it and, frankly, I am quite good at it. But it has occurred to me that maybe I should also use my knowledge to help people."

"You want to be a teacher?"

"Possibly. But first I have to do some more learning."

"You want me to buy you a school?" Wade said.

"Wade, you did win the largest New York Lottery ever, but don't spend it all in one place. I would, however, like you to loan me the money so I can go back to Loyola and finish my degree."

"You got it. Anything else?"

"Well, I've never mentioned this to Dee before, but I have been thinking of starting my own business for a while now. You've made your fortune; I'd like another loan so I can start working towards mine."

"Sure!" Wade said. "I'll give you whatever you want."

"Not give, loan," Stewart said. "With interest."

Then he thought for a moment about the enormity of $115 million.

"Low interest," he said. "Very low to radically low interest. Biblically low."

Wade clapped his hand on Stewart's shoulder.

"Is that all you want, brother?" Wade said. "No problem."

"Don't get me wrong. I want to pay a fair amount. But just sort of a diminished rate, an anemic shadow of a banker's fee—a waif of an interest charge."

"A-OK," Wade answered. "What kind of business are you going to open?"

Stewart was silent.

"Come on," Wade said. "I'm family."

"I'm afraid it's not very glamorous or exciting."

"I'm probably thinking it's something ten times less glamorous and exciting than it actually is."

"I don't think it is possible to get ten times less glamorous or exciting," Stewart said. "But I want to open a hardware store."

He had always loved hardware stores, to which he was a frequent visitor. He saw them as oases of order and remedy, of possibility and repair in a confused and broken world. If one lived simply enough, was there any problem a compatible washer, an accommodating length of fencing, the properly sized toggle bolt, or enough fresh lumber could not set right?

"Money to open your own hardware store and to go to school. Check," Wade said. "Can you think of anything else you'd like?" Wade asked.

"How much money do you have on you right now?" Stewart asked.

"Charlene made a withdrawal this afternoon, before we knowed we won," Wade said. "I think about twenty-five dollars or so."

"May I have a one-dollar bill?" Stewart asked.

"Certainly," Wade said, pulling some coiled bills from his jeans pocket.

Stewart took the bill in both hands, kissed George Washington's image and then began to methodically rip it into tiny pieces. He cupped the torn pieces in one hand and then threw them in the air above him.

"I've always wanted to do that," he said.

Wade grinned incredulously and handed Stewart another bill.

"Oh, a fiver. Nice, hello Abe. Stewart took the bill, rolled it into a tight cigarette and stuck it in his mouth. Wade patted the top of the step until his hand made contact with Charlene's lighter. He brought the lighter's tiny flame before Stewart's face and lit the end of the bill. Stewart took a drag and let out an exultant stream of bluish green smoke.

"Did you know this is illegal?" Stewart said. "They actually have laws against burning currency. Was this ever a real problem? Juveniles seeing people do it in the movies and then skipping school to torch their piggy banks?"

Wade tittered as he fashioned a ten-dollar bill into a little ash tray, which he held in the palm of his hand.

"Oh, thanks," Stewart said, tapping the end of the ember

against the edge of the bowl. "Police said if they had not arrived in time, the man may have burned all the money in the vault," he intoned. "Alex Hunter, Channel 8—the news watcher."

Wade reached between his feet for the bottle of champagne. The cork popped off and went sailing into the night sky. White bubbles rose out of the top of the bottle and ran onto his hand. He put his mouth to the bottle like a suckling and caught the flow of rising foam in his mouth. He held the champagne in the pouch of his inflated cheeks for a moment and then spat it out onto the lawn. He took another drink and spat it out also. A third time he lifted the bottle high against his lips and his cheeks ballooned more extravagantly than ever. He moved the bottle aside and sent a long, thin stream of liquid between his front teeth, arcing it into the dark air. Stewart gazed at this, the smoldering cigarette bill hanging loosely between his lips. When the stream ran short and drippled down his chin, Wade turned and smirked at Stewart.

"I always wanted to do that," he said. He took a deep breath and then another long draw from the bottle and let the contents fall from his mouth and onto the concrete between his shoes.

"I'm getting out of breath, man."

He turned the bottle upside down and the liquid gurgled out onto the ground near the yucca plant.

"Tomorrow, I'll see how Auntie Gin holds up against gravity," Wade said, moving his hand as if he were emptying another bottle.

Stewart flicked the bill out into the direction of the champagne.

"Yes, no more smoking money for me, either," he said. "But, Wade, that is going to be a lot harder than picking those winning numbers."

"I know it," Wade said. "But I got to do it. I want my mind back full-time to enjoy all this."

He pushed the bottle off the steps. It fell with a soft clinking sound against the pea gravel surrounding the yucca. Both men's glances fell out towards their sleeping families.

"I want to see them kids grow up and not just think I remember seeing them grow up or wished I had. You see, man, I got another pair of winning numbers."

He showed Stewart a plain white business card. The name William J. Halven was written in the center of the card and below it a single word—counselor.

"That's the man that helped me at the church in Biloxi. I was four weeks without a drink—thirty days, nights, too. I almost got a token. I think I want to go back and get that token. Because, really, those wives and them kids out there, they're all we got."

"I know it," Stewart said. "They're all we'll ever have."

Both men were silent for a time. Wade was the first to move off the steps.

"Come on, bro. Let's go take care of our families," he said.

Chapter 34

The following day the national news descended upon the Georges' home in search of Wade. When a reporter from NBC learned that Wade, in fact, lived in the small addition to the main house with his wife and four children and that the dwelling had concrete floors and homemade quilts for walls, the wires sang with stories of the poverty-stricken Southern family blessed by the benevolence of chance in faraway New York.

The quote "I never even been to New York," found its way into numerous stories in various forms in what became the feel-good story of the moment. Charlene and the children soon joined the spotlight in front of flashing cameras and jostling, jotting reporters. Being the one whose birthdate was part of the winning combination and the one who was present when the winning ticket was purchased, Dwight became an instant focus of attention.

One picture of him being held aloft by a grinning Wade and the caption, "Winning Boy!" made the papers as far away as Great Britain. In the meanwhile, Stewart worked furiously on the addition, trying to erect at least one inner wall before another crew filmed the family seated on the dusty cement floor in front of one of Charlene's quilts.

Charlene was interviewed for a special Sunday feature in the *Times-Picayune* on how it felt to be suddenly and fabulously rich. Dee, being the first to hear the good news, was interviewed by the archdiocesan paper the *Clarion Herald*. An inventive writer there confected a Mary/ Elizabeth relationship between Dee and Charlene with Dee's "newly discovered child perhaps leaping with joy in her womb upon hearing of the great gift from heaven's horn of plenty."

All four of the children were featured on a local kid's Saturday morning show. They told a host, who dressed like a cowboy and introduced cartoons drawn twenty years before the kids were born, what they planned to do with their inheritances. The back of Stewart's head and shoulders were caught in the background of the photograph of Charlene and Dee for the Mary and Elizabeth story. He was straightening a painting that had wavered just a fraction of an inch to one side of the wall behind the seated women. The painting had been placed there a few seconds before by Stewart to cover some perceived blemish on the wall. The painting was of a succulent green yucca plant on a velvet desert.

When Wade returned home from New York, he was wearing a dark blue suit with latent silver pin stripes. A red tie was pulled close against his shirt by a gold clasp. His hair had been combed, parted on the side, and finally pulled off his forehead. An exaggerated "Whoaaaah!" arose from those seated at the kitchen table as he walked through the front door of the Georges' home.

"They made me wear this, y'all," Wade said, smirking shyly.

The table around which the family sat was covered with newspaper and heaped in the center with boiled blue crabs. Extra leaves had been inserted to expand the table and Tim, Amy, Karmen, and Edward had joined the gathering.

"Wade, this is Edward," Dee said. "Tim and Amy's father."

Wade stepped forward, switching a satchel into his left hand and offering his right. Edward remained seated and showed both palms, which were covered with the yellow paste of crab fat.

"Sorry," he said. "But nice to meet you."

"Have a crustacean," Stewart said, sucking the end of an orange claw.

Karmen cracked a crab's body in half and spiced water squirted out of its broken shell directly into Stewart's face.

"Ahhhh," Stewart said, grabbing a napkin and pressing it into his eye.

Amy, Tim, and the four children tittered appreciatively. Karmen looked up crimson and stunned. These crabs were strange animals to him, and one had just gone off in his hands.

Wade pulled out a chair next to Charlene and sat with both hands resting on top of his satchel.

"So how was New York?" Stewart asked.

"Not as bad as they say," Wade answered.

"We saw you on TV," Amy said, lifting out of her seat and grabbing a crab from the heap.

"Save some for the children, Aim," Edward said.

"There's plenty more in the pot," Dee countered from the other end of the table. "Have all you'd like. Karmen, have you figured out how to eat these yet?"

Karmen was pinching tiny bits of white meat out of the broken shell.

"Oh, yes," he said. "They're very good."

He was starving to death. These things had about as much meat in them as rocks. He had already eaten six packs of the crackers that Dee had set out to accompany the crabs. His eyes surreptitiously roved the table for more. Wade touched his tie self-consciously and felt a compress of sweat around the collar of his shirt.

"Cashed the first check yet?" Stewart asked.

Wade smirked again.

"With an expired out-of-state license in a Manhattan bank," Wade said.

"Guess they must watch the television, too," Edward

said. "Jane Pauley as cute in person as she is on TV?"

"Cuter," Wade said and sent a sheepish glance towards Charlene.

"Where's your luggage?" Dee asked.

"Traffic as bad as they say?" Tim asked.

"Me and David and Dwight were on television," Darren said. "Did you see us, Daddy?"

"How many interviews have you done so far?

"Had a chance to sightsee while you were there?"

"Layover long?"

"Glad to be home?"

"Do you know a Tom Newhouse? He called three times."

"Didn't get mugged, did you?"

Wade answered each question as well as he was able. Often, they came at the same time and the two questioners would look at each other and begin to answer the other's question themselves. Often Wade did not know the answer to the question, or had forgotten, or before he could get the answer out, the questioner answered his own question and went on to announce it to the rest of the table.

"Are you feeling alright?" Charlene asked.

The table fell silent.

"Fine," Wade said, unconvincingly. "I'd just like to take a ride for a few minutes if I could. Alone."

"But you just got in," Charlene said.

"I know, but I need to take care of a few things."

He looked around the table apologetically.

"I won't be long. It's only two in the afternoon. I'll be home before dark."

His fingernails clicked nervously on the edge of the satchel as he spoke. He rose abruptly and walked to the door. After he exited, everyone in the room was completely silent except for Karmen, who broke open an orange and white claw and widened his eyes at the unexpected plug of meat within.

"Whoa ho! Look at that!" he said triumphantly.

But no one was listening.

Chapter 35

The Buick bounced and buckled over the oyster shell drive that ran behind The Trader's Lounge. The front axle of the car scooped up handfuls of the shells and sent them back, rattling along its underside. The car came to a stop astride a low mound of shells beneath an oak tree. Ted was resting against the base of the tree, his bandanna pulled over his forehead and nearly covering his eyes. His head was thrown back. His mouth was wide open. On the blanket before him was a half-eaten box of fried chicken and a fully drunk bottle of vodka. Wade looked at the man through the windshield of his car for nearly a full minute. Both of his hands were clasping the top of the steering wheel.

"Can't go back," he said.

He held his stare but took one hand off the steering wheel and found the inside handle of the car's door. He exited the car and walked to the edge of the old man's blanket. He took a drumstick out of the box and plugged it into the opened mouth. For a moment, the drumstick sat upright in the orifice, with the man's wheezing breath finding an outlet around the edges of the chicken. Then his breathing became irregular and, finally, clogged. Wade snatched the drumstick away. The old man coughed and gagged, and his head fell forward.

"Hey now—" he said, holding a hand to his throat and looking at Wade through watery eyes.

"Get up, you fool," Wade said to him.

The old man squinted up at the suited figure that stood before him.

"Who's there? The cops? I ain't done nothing, sir. I'm just setting here resting,"

"It's me," Wade said. "The name is Wade Terry. I may have told you that a hundred times or I may have never told you it before. I can't remember. Now what's your name?"

The old man looked closer and then a mild light of recognition spread across his face.

"Oh, yeah," he said. "Theodore L. Silva. That's my name."

"Your friends call you Theodore?" Wade asked.

The old man let out one of his bursting laughs.

"Young man, I don't have any friends and neither do you. So why don't you give me whatever liquid you're carrying for a few of these spare parts," he indicated the box of chicken, "And we'll leave the names to the painters."

He nodded toward the red and blue graffiti sprayed on one of the walls that bordered the drive.

"Can I call you Ted?" Wade said. He squatted in front of the old man.

"A nattily dresser, today, ain't we?" the old man observed. "Yes, Ted is fine. Whatever pleases you. Neither of us will remember."

Wade picked up one of the rough oyster shells, turned it over in his hand and noted the beautiful blue-gray swirl of its inner side. He weighed the shell, bouncing it slightly in one hand and then threw it against a section of the graffiti. The shell scattered and ricocheted, leaving a white, chalky hummock against the wall.

"Ted, I think I need your help," Wade said.

"Help for what?" the old man said.

"Come on, I'll show you."

Wade took hold of Ted's arm and began to lift him towards the car. The old man stayed put and brushed him away.

"Where you think you're taking me?" he said.

"I'm taking you home to live with me and my wife and all the children I am always mumbling about in the night," Wade said. "I won the lottery last week—$115 million. Now, I got more friends than I can count, but I want you to be the one I can count on."

"Well, hold on," the old said. "What if I don't want to go? Don't I have my rights?"

Wade stood up.

"Sure. Fine then. Live under this tree all your life, eating garbage and drinking any stranger's poison. Drag me down with you, if you can."

Wade turned and began walking towards the car. He had only taken two steps when the old man called out to him.

"Well, what if I told you I like living under this tree and eating garbage?"

Wade turned around and looked at him.

"Then you've got problems $115 million, and a best friend couldn't solve," he said. "Or you're a lying drunk."

Wade continued to walk away.

"How do I know you won a lottery," Ted countered. "How do I know you ain't the craziest drunk liar I ever seen?"

Wade tuned around once more.

"If you haven't read the papers or seen the TV, you don't. But does a crazy, drunk liar do this?"

He took a money clip from his vest pocket and pulled from it a stiff one-hundred-dollar bill. He methodically stripped the bill into shreds and let the pieces fall on the wind. The old man reached out his hands as if to catch the falling treasure and then looked at Wade thunderstruck.

"That's the last time I'm going to do that. Ever. If you want any further proof, you'll have to talk to my wife and kids," Wade said.

He strode briskly to the Buick and started the engine. Ted rose quickly, kicking his blanket aside. He stopped a few feet short of entering the car and instead peered through the open window of the passenger side.

"But I'm a crazy old man," he told Wade. "People might think you're strange if you have me for a best friend."

"I know," Wade said.

"They might start talking and saying you ain't nothing but a drunk and a bum yourself, after all, even if you got all that money."

"I know, "Wade said.

The old man looked to either side of him, as if he were about to cross a busy intersection.

"Hang on boy, I been down so long I might not know how to live up. I might not be able to give up the cheap liquid. I might not know how to take a bath every night or even talk to nice people."

"I know," said Wade.

"And you still don't care?" Ted queried.

"Yes, I still do care," Wade said. "Once you realize that the terrible knowledge you and I been drinking to forget isn't that terrible at all, you'll care too. Once you realize that there's not such a far space between up and down and top and bottom— that it's only an inch, if it's even an inch—you'll care too."

"Listen to the philosophy," Ted said and spritely walked the remaining steps to the car door. "Open up, Wade," he said.

Wade leaned over and opened the door from the inside. Ted settled down comfortably among the vinyl and earthy smells of the car.

"First time I rode in the front seat of a car in a long time," he said.

"You'll get used to it, Ted. This is the first time I've driven sober in one in a long time."

They drove over the tumbling plains of oyster shells at a steady pace.

"And I think I know your wife's name. Charlene," Ted said. "And the kids are . . . Darren, David, Dwight and . . ."

"Jude," Wade said. "The youngest."

"Jude?" Ted said. "You was always yelling out Hope."

Wade checked to make sure the way was clear before pulling out of the oyster shell drive for the last time.

"Yes," he said. "I guess I was."

Chapter 36

Stewart sat at a desk in the middle of the living room working a stencil pattern over a piece of white poster board he had laid against its surface. Lately, he had preferred to work here in this wider, taller room rather than in the confines of their bedroom where furniture, the bed, and clothes competed for the limited space. Dee appeared in the periphery of his vision.

"Charlene and I are going to the mall," she said. "Do you need anything?"

Stewart kept his eyes on his work. He thought he had just shaded the wrong letter with his indelible marker.

"Huh, uh, no, honey," he said. "Be careful."

Just beginning her fifth month, Dee had already expanded greatly and had acquired a Charlie Chaplin-esque stride. She unhooked a set of keys from a rack and padded out the door.

Moments later, Stewart lifted the completed poster off the surface of the desk and admired it with satisfaction. The surface of the paper was slightly creased in areas by the weight of the artist's hand but, for the most part, the message: "Please, Help Yourself to Paint Samples," was splendid. The poster would be placed on the wall above an aluminum rack, offering slips of paper bearing multiple shades of available paint color. This rack would be placed to the left of the store's main counter, next to a cardboard hamper filled with inexpensive brushes. Stewart studied the arrangement in his mind, savoring each vivid detail, until a rap at the front door brought him back to the present. He watched the doorknob turn and saw Sid, in his postal uniform, peer around the corner of the door.

"Anybody home?" he called. He was looking toward the stairs.

"Over here, Sid," Stewart said.

Sid turned with a raised chin and smiled a greeting toward Stewart.

"Where y'at, you old pensioner?" he said, closing the door behind him.

Stewart took his hand and shook it warmly.

"When did they switch you to route four?" he asked.

"As soon as they made up their minds. You know how Gravier is," Sid said.

"Well, how is it as far as a route goes? I've lived in this house almost all my life but never delivered to it once," Stewart said.

Sid was sifting through his bag for the Georges' mail.

"Not bad," he said. "Except for a collie on Voisin. A big, hairy, vicious thing. Lassie's evil twin. The owner said it used to just love the old mailman."

Sid looked at the poster that Stewart had leaned against the desk.

"I would have taken the money and run," Sid said.

Stewart blushed a bit.

"Well."

"So, when's the business opening up?" Sid asked, easing one haunch on the edge of a nearby settee.

"Soon. Couple months—probably early next year. We have a few odds and ends to put together," Stewart said. He waved a fan of pamphlets advertising various types of power tools before Sid.

"Tell me you couldn't do some serious remodeling or repair with these. Look at those crisp cords and sparkling blades."

"Keep those away from my wife," Sid said. "I'd rather buy jewelry."

"Hey, Sid," Stewart said, suddenly. "Have I shown you this? Look what I made."

His palms were outstretched toward the desk.

"You made a desk calendar," Sid said.

"No. I made the desk. All by myself. From the first nail to the final coat."

Sid stood up from the settee and took a step toward the desk for a better view.

"I didn't know you—"

"I didn't either," Stewart said. "I just started doing it and it all fell into place."

Sid scrutinized the desk. It was made of oak and stained a dark, textured hue. The craftmanship was flawless.

"You didn't follow anyone's pattern?" Sid asked.

"No, just the one I had in my head. I used to think the hardware business was about repairing and mending. But it's about making, too. Not everything in this world is broken."

They talked for several more minutes, but as he spoke Stewart noticed Sid's eyes wandering over the desk, studying every inch of it. He was fairly transfixed by it.

"Better be shoving off," he said finally. "That collie will be getting hungry by this time."

Stewart moved from behind the desk. Sid held up a hand.

"I know the way out. Thanks. Here, maybe I will take some of these pamphlets. It'll give me something to read on my lunch break."

"No longer reading other people's magazines before you deliver them?" Stewart asked, handing him the stack of pamphlets.

"I'm all caught up for this month," Sid said. "And the good postcards don't start coming in for another couple of weeks."

"I never read one in all my years on the job," Stewart called to him as he walked through the door. "You hear me? Not one."

Stewart allowed the residue of a smile to linger on his face as he settled back down behind the desk. Sometime in the late afternoon, a block of bright sun fell upon the desk.

Wade was standing in the open doorway.

"Brother, come out here, quick," he said and closed the door.

For the last hour, Stewart had been aware of some vague excitement outside, hushed admonitions and scurrying. He had dismissed it as some game with complex, arbitrary rules requiring secret oaths for admission—a game the neighborhood children had concocted and were carrying out in the street before his house, perhaps spilling onto his lawn, perhaps not. It was hard to say because someone had closed the shutters on the front windows. Now, there was a sudden silence following Wade's departure. Stewart rose from the desk and walked towards the door.

When he opened the door, he was blinded by the sun. Not one sun but nine gleaming shafts of light. Nine swords. The Knights were in formation before him in the uniforms that had stayed sealed inside the church office since the debacle at Presentation Day. Their drawn swords were held aloft like sterling torches. Wade approached the steps and handed Stewart a megaphone. A real megaphone with an inflexible handle in the center of it and "St. Andrew" printed on it in letters that began small and grew larger and larger until the final "w" was six times bigger than the first "s."

"I had to give you something you didn't have to pay back," Wade said and moved away from the steps.

Behind Wade, Stewart spotted Charlene leaning against the side of her brand-new minivan. She wore white pants and a blue and white striped sailor's shirt. Her hair was still long but it was parted on the side and emboldened by a soft body wave. She wore thin wrist bracelets that rang together with each gesture of her hand and golden earrings in the shape of sailboats. She looked beautiful.

The great sliding door of the van was open and there sat Dee and the twins, Dwight, and the baby, all wearing bright, new vacation clothes. Tim, Amy, and Karmen sat on the grass below them, Karmen furtively holding Amy's hand and wearing one of the old stocking ties for a headband. Next to him was Edward and Ted. The old man was still dressed in his usual garb, only his clothes were washed, and his eyes jingled, as if they were seeing everything for the first time.

"Return swords," Stewart said through the megaphone.

The swords slid into the sheaths with a gilt-edged finality.

Stewart took the megaphone away from his mouth. He looked at the Knights and then at his family.

"Our Lady was born and grew up in the village of Nazareth," he said, again speaking through the megaphone. His voice sounded singular and close.

"Sometimes, the people who lived there were very good and walked with God and other times they could hurt one another very deeply. They were like us. They often forgot that all the Lord really expected of them was to love Him and their brother."

He looked at Wade for a long moment, nodded and then

readjusted the megaphone over his mouth. In a clear and confident voice, he began to sing "Ave Maria." The words floated into the surrounding streets of the neighborhood. The Knights began to slide forward in graceful strides toward the altar that was a home. Stewart's song was uninterrupted by either direction or comment. For it occurred to him that in this life he had talked long and loudly, but had not sung nearly enough.